RAW

DECEPTION

RISING STAKES SCREENPLAY SERIES

NIKHIL KAMKOLKAR

RAW
Deception

Nikhil Kamkolkar

Copyright © 2025 by Nikhil Kamkolkar

Rising Stakes Screenplay Series™ is a trademark of Kamkol Productions LLC

KAMKOL
Kamkol titles may be purchased in bulk for educational, business, promotional or training use. Inquiries should be addressed to nikhil@kamkol.com

Identifiers
ISBN 978-1-970338-04-1 (paperback)
ISBN 978-1-970338-05-8 (hardcover)

CONTENTS

ONE
ADVENTURES IN SILENCE

You know what's a real bitch?

Not sleeping for three days straight.

That's when I become the nastiest SOB ever to have an overweight man gasping for air in a chokehold, his brain struggling to instruct his desperate hands to grab my Glock.

Then the SOB stopped wriggling and reached for my eyes instead. Damn. Guess his brain was getting some oxygen after all.

I shifted my hold, leaned my head, so that his searching fingers entered my open mouth.

I bit down. Hard.

He screamed.

I tightened my chokehold so the sound stayed stuck in his throat. That's how it would have ended if it wasn't for that goddamn phone call.

I recognized the ringtone on my cell phone. How could that be? That ringtone was assigned to the only person on this planet who mattered to me.

Priyanka. My wife. My dead wife.

She was murdered and I was hot on the trail of those who killed her.

The man started pointing at my pocket from where the cellphone rang. Why would a man about to die want me to take a call?

My curiosity peaked. I figure curiosity is a bigger son of a bitch than lack of sleep.

I loosened my grip, allowing my new friend a life-saving breath.

Maybe it was the rogue unit within RAW, I speculated.

Stop. What the fuck is RAW, you ask?

THE RESEARCH AND ANALYSIS WING—RAW—IS India's intelligence arm, like the CIA in the U.S. or Saudi Arabia's GIP.

People dismiss it as primitive, ineffective. We let them.

A mask of ineptitude to hide what we can actually do.

Those who knew, knew—and some of them are out to dismantle RAW, and the one unit inside it that does the work India needs most.

The Chanakya Division.

Named for the ancient strategist, the Chanakya Division—"Chaks," if you're family—runs on an informal lattice. A matrix of handlers and teams working independently; missions rarely touch. Sounds insane. It isn't. It's the only way to contain leaks and keep India secure.

Our world is anything but secure. Double agents at every turn.

Chaks doesn't chase terrorists. We tell the world that's what we do.

Our mission is to hunt down corruption.

Corruption hollows a nation from the inside—more dangerous than any bomb with a manifesto.

It was this corruption that had led this overweight, out-of-breath gentle-man, into my loving embrace.

I SHOVED Fat Man away and took the phone out of my pocket. Watched him as he hit the wall and slipped down to the floor. I trained my Glock on him out of habit, looking around to make sure we stayed out of sight in this isolated area at the Bangalore airport.

Now, this is counter intuitive to so many people and worth explaining. When you take in information, you expose yourself to dis-information. This phone could be like a virus that placed verbal manipulators expertly designed to lead my cognitive machinery down a path I should not be on. The last time I let that happen, I lost my wife. I lost my best friend.

I put the phone to my ear. Not saying a word. The voice on the other end called out my name.

"Abhay?"

I didn't ask who it was. I already knew.

It was my dead wife. It was Priyanka.

TWO
MY MALLU FRIEND

THREE DAYS EARLIER

Tony and I were cruising back to my place in his Maruti when my phone chimed with that obnoxious ringtone everyone hated, but never failed to make me grin.

Tony rolled his eyes. "That's annoying."

I winked at him and picked up. "Hi babe!"

Tony pretended to look out the window, but I knew he was all ears. We were trained that way. Listening was our bread and butter.

"Where are you?" she asked.

Her voice had an edge that sent shivers down my spine. I was in tune with every nuance of Priyanka's voice, and I caught the raw terror she tried to mask.

"They're going to kill me," she said, flat and emotionless.

I didn't waste time asking questions. They didn't matter.

I tried to match her cool. "Let me talk to them. They won't kill you. You'll be fine."

I glanced at Tony. Wordlessly, he floored the accelerator, zigzagging through midday traffic toward home.

"Priyanka?" All I heard was dead air.

We arrived at my flat in the swanky Serenity Grove in New Mumbai to find the door ajar. No forced entry.

We entered, guns drawn.

The living room was spotless, just as Priyanka liked it. No sign of a struggle. Her oil paintings of ruby-throated hummingbirds – a tribute to our time in New York – hung on the walls. Mute witnesses to whatever had happened here.

I could hear Tony panting from sprinting up five flights of stairs. Kids playing cricket outside. Traffic.

I turned every corner, expecting to see Priyanka's bloodied body. But there was no one in the apartment. Priyanka was gone.

Taken.

TONY PUT his arm around me as I stood there, shattered. Angry. Confused. If I couldn't protect my wife, how could I protect my country? I forced myself to focus on the facts. The next steps.

Tony suggested calling RAW's Site Investigation Team, but I refused. No RAW. No police.

A kidnapped spouse compromised an agent, and RAW would bench me until she was found. That was the last thing I wanted. I needed to stay in the game to chase her captors.

We scoured the flat for clues, but we knew the kidnappers were pros who wouldn't leave a trace. Imagine my shock when I found a cellphone on the bed with a note underneath:

"Your wife dies tonight."

Not if I get to you first, assholes.

Tony checked the phone for explosives using his portable detector. It wasn't foolproof, but it gave us some peace of mind.

We left the flat, cellphone in hand – my sole link to my vanished wife – and headed to Bandra.

"What now?" Tony asked.

I knew the call with impossible demands would come soon. I had to act fast.

"Sheru," I said.

Tony nodded. If anyone knew about a professional kidnapping team in Mumbai, it was Sheru, kingpin of the city's underworld.

Tony expertly navigated through the chaos of Indian cars, weaving in and out of traffic. Soon, we left South Mumbai behind.

What would I do without my Mallu buddy, I wondered.

Fireworks lit up the night sky. Diwali, the festival of lights and Hindu New Year, was tonight.

I considered myself spiritual, not religious. Most Hindus like me only get religious past sixty, when mortality stares us down.

"We're being followed!" Tony's sharp voice interrupted my thoughts.

Tony pointed at the TATA Sumo Mumbai Police Interceptor tailing us in the rearview mirror. It kept its distance, but it was there.

"They must have followed us from the apartment," I suggested.

"No, it's the phone," Tony replied. "They must have a tracker in it, or they're triangulating the cell signal."

I eyed the device I was holding, tempted to toss it. But the phone was my lifeline to Priyanka. They'd probably banked on that. They wanted to keep tabs on us, see where we went, who we met. Keep us company. Nice bunch.

"Let's say hello," Tony grinned.

I couldn't help but smile. Tony swerved onto a side road, and sure enough, the TATA Sumo followed, maintaining its distance. They didn't seem concerned about being spotted.

Tony pulled to a stop. "Follow me," he said tersely. I knew my brain was fried, so I trusted my Mallu friend and his plan.

I followed him without question.

That was my first mistake.

THREE
DIWALI DHAMAKA

THE BANG-BANG-BANG SYMPHONY of a thousand-bomb Ladi crescendoed as we neared the nondescript building. A dirt-streaked tin sign declared it to be the 'H.M.O. Water Society'. Tony was familiar with the place; I wasn't.

"Go in and wait. I'll outflank them—there's a side entrance," Tony shouted at me, his voice tense. I followed his instructions.

That was my mistake number two. I should've stayed with Tony.

The police interceptor screeched to a halt nearby. I saw three men jump out. It didn't take much to figure out who their leader was. A fair-skinned man I immediately nicknamed "Goru." He was the one barking orders.

They spotted me and Goru sent his goons charging after me. I dashed inside. I wished I had gotten a better sense from Tony about what his plan was.

I entered the building and saw two elderly female security guards chatting and laughing. The building was closed for the holiday and they really shouldn't have been there.

I waved my Glock at them and yelled, "Police! Building's closed! Go home!" They exchanged a fearful glance and scrambled out a side door.

I raced through a narrow corridor and entered a room with a sign outside -- "Customer Service." Perfect. It was littered with archaic telephones. What a set for a shootout. I prepped my weapon, checked my spare mag and found a spot from where I could cover all the entrances.

I could anticipate the action several steps ahead in my mind. And I was prepared to improvise.

More than anything, I had faith in my mallu friend.

This was my third mistake.

DIWALI FIRECRACKERS ROARED like battle drums, signaling a war between good and evil. As I prepped for my own bang-bangs, the phone from Priyanka's kidnappers rang.

The caller ID simply read "Unavailable", and I knew it had to be Goru. I half-expected the whole thing would explode like a Laxmi bomb in my face when I answered the call.

I pressed the green button.

No explosion. Good.

The voice on the other end was surprisingly deep. "We have your friend."

I heard Tony yell in the background - "Abhay, they'll kill you!"

The deep voice offered a clarifying note: "meet us on the roof or we kill your friend."

The sounds of the Diwali firecrackers faded from my mind. I quickly weighed my options and took the stairs to the roof.

Glock held in a two-handed grip I reached the rooftop. My mind was a mix of fear and determination.

I stepped out onto the roof, it was empty. No Tony. No Goru.

That's when I heard the explosion. That wasn't a Diwali firecracker. That was the sound of a fuel tank exploding.

I rushed to the parapet wall and looked over.

My car, the one we had arrived in, was now a fiery inferno.

That phone rang again. I answered.

Goru said in his taunting voice, "your friend's dead and burning in your car."

The words were like a physical blow, and I raised my Glock in fury, taking aim at the Interceptor.

But Goru's next words froze my trigger pull. "Your wife is with us."

Priyanka's head was pushed out of the window of the Interceptor for a moment, as if to see what I would do.

Then, she was pulled back in.

The Interceptor accelerated away. I held my fire. I couldn't hold my tears.

As I stood there frozen, unable to decide a course of action, I heard Priyanka's scream on the phone.

"Abhay!"

Followed by the sound of gunfire.

Goru's voice, "and now, your wife is dead too."

The phone went dead. So did I.

The exploding fireworks around me no longer spoke. They were mute witnesses to this moment in which my world was forever changed.

There was no thought of revenge. Not yet. That'd come later. All I could think of right now was why. Why did this happen? Why Priyanka? Who was Goru? Why?

I didn't know.

All I knew was that my mallu friend was dead.

Priyanka was dead.

And I was no longer living.

FOUR
MORNING RAGAS

I KNEW I should feel something, but I was numb.

I made calls. My personal network was looking for any information about Priyanka's body that I knew they would dump somewhere. Any information that could lead me to Goru, the man I held responsible for her murder.

My relationship with Priyanka had been strained in the weeks leading up to her death.

She seemed distracted and distant, stressed out about something but she wouldn't say what. I couldn't shake the feeling that her stress was connected to her abduction.

Now it didn't matter. All that mattered was finding Goru and making him pay for what he did.

My anger ebbed, allowing grief to swell.

I drank.

It was early morning when sleep began to overcome me and Priyanka's alarm clock went off. It played her favorite track by Pandit Bhimsen Joshi. His distinctive vocals were accompanied by her voice in my head telling me all about the nuances of the Hindustani classical track playing, and how Ahir Bhairav was her favorite raga ever.

The haunting melodies stirred up feelings within me. Loneliness. Uncertainty. But hope and determination as well.

I felt energy surging through me. An ancient energy that reached through time to connect me to the vast human experience that had gone before me.

It was a feeling I wish I could have shared with Priyanka.

It was late morning when Ram Chandra, a close friend in the National Analytics and Security Services, called. He had a location for me. A call had been made on the cell phone two days before it was left in my apartment.

The location was in a temporary marketplace for fireworks erected just for the Diwali season organized by the Sri Durga Fireworks Association.

I jumped on my trusty Enfield Bullet. Its deep throated sound resonating with the sound of my heart pounding.

The market was off a major road and surrounded by commercial establishments. Traffic was picking up, so I jumped on the Ring Road for a portion of the ride to avoid it.

Twenty minutes later, I reached, and was running to the shop when

I saw him.

Goru, wearing a bright yellow shirt had already seen me. When I spotted him, he was just standing there, watching me.

Our eyes met and the bastard smirked.

I exploded with anger and raced to smash his face in. He took off, jumping over tables like he was a goddamn parkour artist.

I stayed on his tail as he raced through the crowded market and shoving people aside.

A furious store owner, cursed after us both -- "what the fuck do you think you are doing, motherfucker? I'll break your balls and feed them to you for dinner" – throwing a box of "Thunder Bombs" at our fleeing backs in a futile gesture.

Someone or something tripped me. I fell.

When I got back up, Goru was nowhere to be seen. As my eyes searched for him, a fire started at a stall where I had seen him last and fireworks started going off.

It was chaos.

Goru must have started the fire. I raced towards that stall and saw the hole ripped in the fabric at the back.

I ran through the fire and jumped through the hole.

I heard a motorbike roar off to my right.

It was Goru. I ran behind him. But it was no use. Within moments, he was gone.

I grit my teeth. I would stop at nothing to find Goru. Make him pay for what he did to Priyanka.

This was just the beginning of my hunt.

FIVE
ASHES TO ASHES, DUST TO DUST

PRIYANKA WOULD HAVE BEEN CREMATED. But there was no body to cremate.

Tony had no body left to speak of. A funeral home did the best it could do to gather his remains into a casket which I then flew to Bengaluru.

Tony had no family of his own, but his parents, brother and two sisters attended. They wanted a quick burial. Tony never spoke of them. They didn't feel much of a connection to Tony from what I could see.

Soon it was all over.

Tony, my mallu friend, was resting for all of eternity six feet below.

It was time to get back to my mission.

I spent the rest of the day planting seeds I hoped would result in a harvest of kills.

I hopped on a flight to Delhi.

Running into the dead ends made me realize I needed help. I had to see if the organization I had dedicated my life to, would help me in my quest for justice.

Vengeance. My quest for vengeance.

The agency car picked me up. A Toyota Innova with darkened windows. I slipped into the front passenger seat and closed my eyes.

I had to focus my mind for the conversation I was about to face.

I couldn't do it. With a sigh, I opened my eyes and saw the driver watching me in the rearview mirror.

"What's your name?" I asked.

"Nihal Khan", he responded with a smile.

"Nice name. What does it mean?"

"I was given the name, not its meaning," was his matter-of-fact response.

Nihal, probably feeling bad for his blunt response, spoke up. "What's your name, sir?"

"Abhay."

"Fearless. Your name means fearless. Are you fearless?" Nihal Khan asked with no malice.

I wanted to say yes, but the answer was no.

I had a deep fear of enclosed spaces which always triggered a deep-set panic reaction. No, I was not fearless. But I had hidden that fact well from the rest of the world.

Except perhaps from Nihal, as he proceeded to answer his own question. "I don't think you are fearless. You look like a person who fears a lot of things."

"Thank you, Nihal," I responded. The sarcasm in my voice was lost on him.

He proceeded to tell me his life story - his move from his village in Uttar Pradesh to Delhi to find work, his initial stints as a driver driving the very old Premier Padmini cabs to his job with the agency.

I nodded absently. My mind was finally cooperating and I was working out what I was going to say to my Handler, and more importantly, Chief.

———

CHIEF KEPT his focus on the pen he twirled in his fingers. He said nothing after I had finished.

My handler Jacob, on the timid side when it came to managerial situations, wasn't about to break the heavy silence.

I decided not to either.

We sat there. Three mute men.

Chief sighed before he broke the uncomfortable silence. "Hiding information from the SIT team is stupid and illegal and a firable offense."

Chief wasn't so insensitive as to add that it may have cost me the lives of my wife and friend. But that thought screamed its way all around the inside of my head.

"Have they found any leads yet?" I enquired, trying to stop hope from creeping into my voice.

"No, not yet..." Chief said. "But your drawing of that Goru fellow is out there now. We have alerted all the authorities to look for Priyanka's body. I'm surprised we haven't found it already."

We sat again in silence.

"I'm recommending you take some time off." Chief saw my protest coming a mile away and cut me off. "I'm ordering you to take some time off. I need you alive."

"Chief, I have to find Priyanka's killers before their trail goes cold."

Chief turned to Jacob who rose up to escort me out of Chief's office.

I knew I had used up all the goodwill I had banked with Chief. I got up and walked out with Jacob.

JACOB and I moved to the cafeteria. Nursing our cups of Chai. "What are you going to do now?" Jacob asked.

"Find Priyanka's killers, find her body."

Jacob was expecting that. But I wasn't expecting his question. "Did you love her, Abhay?"

I hesitated long enough for Jacob to get his answer. I gave him one anyway. "Doesn't matter. She was my wife."

Jacob knew what was going on in my life. He had to or he'd get me killed setting me up with the wrong kind of assignments at the wrong time.

He knew Priyanka and I had grown apart.

"Problems happen in every marriage, but yes, she was your wife." Jacob placed a hand on my shoulder. "I'm sorry about what happened, Abhay. I don't know how to help you. I think taking some time off will help you reconcile with..."

"I don't want to reconcile with anything. I want to kill the killers. That's exactly what I'm going to do."

Jacob shook his head, "you'd be crossing a line, Abhay. Leave it to us, we'll bring them to justice."

Justice.

In India, everything was for sale. Justice more so than anything.

And so, Indians relied on the idea of Karma to offer solace to those who were wronged.

Well, I wasn't going to wait for Karma to deliver justice ten lifetimes from now. I was going to get it in this lifetime.

Jacob sighed. "I have to ask you to hand over your weapon, Abhay. Chief's orders."

"By taking away my gun, you are only making it easier for the enemy to kill me," I said, hoping to convince Jacob to ignore what he had been asked to do.

Jacob had always bent rules for me. But this time, he didn't budge. I unhooked my shoulder holster, and dropped it, with the Glock, on the table.

"I'll have two men assigned to protect you," Jacob added.

"If they can find me, maybe they can protect me," I said, as I walked away.

Gun or no gun, I was on a mission. To find Priyanka's body, find her killer, their boss, their boss's boss and kill them all.

What I did not tell Jacob and Chief was that the kidnappers had left a cell phone for me. I did not want to hand that over.

It was my only link to the killers.

THE EVENING quickly turned into night.

My flight back to Mumbai was delayed due to weather. Finally, we were cleared for takeoff.

From the window of my first class seat, I watched the walkway retreat from the plane, the hydraulics pull the bellows back, and the entire unit roll away.

This crew was on the ball. Mumbai in an hour forty.

The Boeing 737-800 taxied to the end of the runway and turned around for takeoff.

The whine of the engines climaxed and the plane lunged forward. The cabin shook briefly, dancing in the windy turbulence as the wheels left the ground and the plane did easily what it was meant to do.

I too knew what I was meant to do.

Unlike the plane, I had no idea how.

I was experiencing the effect, but had no idea of the cause.

Until I knew that, I'd be flying blind. I tried to empty my mind, hoping that'd give me the nugget I needed to figure this out. All I managed to do was give myself a headache.

As we began our descent in Mumbai, I saw fireworks in the sky still continuing on the day after Diwali.

They looked impotent against the city itself.

Small orange-yellow-green bouquets of erupting fire that barely reached above the buildings and seemed so weak in relation to the incandescence of Mumbai at night.

The Mumbai city tableau moved rapidly underneath us as we flew our approach. The city, a giant beast with its innards exposed, flashed by below us. The pilot delivered a perfect landing.

The steward's voice was calm and bored. "Welcome to Chatrapathi Sivaji International Airport, domestic terminal, Mumbai. The temperature outside is twenty-eight degrees centigrade."

In the terminal, several groups of Muslims waited to board their plane that'd take them on their holy trip to Mecca, or the Haj. One group caught my eye as they huddled in a circle with a mix of the orthodox with their beards and skullcaps, and the modern sporting baseball caps worn backwards. A man in their midst was saying something I could not hear, but the group would nod every so often with a spirited "Ameen!"

I envied them. I envied their faith. I wanted to believe there was a God. I wanted to feel warm and comforted by that thought, as these people clearly were.

The group moved towards the security line and began their journey of light and hopefulness to Mecca.

I began my journey on the road of darkness towards the center of Mumbai.

SIX
WINDLESS ON THE SARGASSO

Calling Salman "my" informer was a joke. Salman informed everyone about everything - for a price. For the right price, he might even tell you the truth. Of course, the truth carried a premium.

Salman's truth was never absolute. It was just a layer of deception removed or an additional motivation brought to light. In our world, "absolute truth" was an oxymoron.

Salman greeted me in his gentle voice, smiling like a man lying on a Caribbean beach sipping a Strawberry Martini. Despite his warm welcome, the distrust between us was real. We hugged like Muslim men do, but the affection was tainted by the world we lived in.

Salman led me to Sheru, the big, bad boss, simply known as Bhai. The one who didn't need his name as a qualifier to the word bhai. It was ironic how a word that meant "brother" in Hindi, became a moniker for criminal dons.

Sheru was a hardcore criminal, and I was not naive to the nature of my work. I realized that in a world where there's light, there must also be darkness. The best we can ever do is choose our darkness.

Maybe it was just my lack of sleep, but as I entered Sheru's lair, my mind raced with the moral equations of my profession.

Sheru's lair was not a specific, fixed, physical place, but it varied from day to day. Plus, there were multiple levels of security that encircled where ever he was at.

It was like entering the Chakravyuha, a hard to penetrate and impossible to exit military formation. Even if one managed to enter the lair to kill Sheru, he wanted to make sure you could never leave it alive, which was the fate the young and dashing Abhimanyu met up with in the epic Mahabharata.

Today, Sheru's lair was the Taj, where Pakistani terrorists had once holed up after their bloody attacks on the streets of Mumbai.

As we pulled into the parking lot, the attendant recognized us and directed us onto a road blocked off for everyone else. Salman's quiet demeanor was a bad sign and if I hadn't counted Sheru among my friends, I would have taken it as a danger sign.

My hand instinctively felt the Glock in the small of my back, offering little assurance as I'd soon have to give it up at the next layer of security.

AT THE CHECKPOINT entering the hotel, Sheru's men swiftly confiscated my gun and handed me a yellow circle with a number printed on it in return. They conducted a thorough physical pat down, probing every inch of my body for implanted weaponry. My balls ached by the time they were done.

We then moved to the elevator bank where three men in full SWAT gear, armed with AK-47s, aimed at us as the doors opened. One was kneeling, while the other two were positioned on either side of the door, ready to set up a cross-fire. They were vulnerable to a grenade attack though, so behind the metal elevator doors was another set of transparent, explosion-resistant doors with holes allowing the AK-47s to fire through. A grenade thrown at these doors would have bounced right back out at the thrower.

More checks. Then the glass door slid open, and I was subjected to another pat down by men dressed in suits.

They led me to the other side of the floor, where I boarded an elevator not available to regular hotel guests. The entire floor permanently booked for Sheru's armed entourage.

As the elevator ascended, I heard a hissing sound.

Gas.

I spotted the nozzle and raced to block it, but another nozzle opened up on the far side of the lift.

"Relax, Abhay," Sheru's voice boomed in the tiny space. "It's only a disinfectant."

Bullshit was my first thought. And my last, for I suddenly dropped to the floor like a tired stone and my eyes shut against my will.

WHEN I REGAINED CONSCIOUSNESS, I found myself bound to a comfortable and classy chair. I kept my eyes closed and pretended to be unconscious, so I could maximize my situational awareness. But my efforts were foiled by an electronic or recorded voice that announced in a soothing American accent, "the subject is awake."

My vitals were being monitored, so there was no fooling anyone.

I opened my eyes and saw Sheru sitting in front of me with a smile on his face. He knew all the tricks of the trade and always found it amusing when he caught one of us trying to fool him.

"Ah, you're awake!" he grinned. "I thought we had lost you to the better world." He approached me and gave me an affectionate slap on the shoulder. "Abhay! How are you, my friend?"

I didn't want to whine, but it came out that way. "Did you have to put me through that gas chamber?"

He laughed in response. "It was fun watching you squirm. For a moment, you thought you were..." He finished the sentence with a typical gesture that captured the essence of a guillotine.

"I had no reason to believe you wouldn't kill me," I retorted.

"Kill a good friend? What kind of man does that?" He burst out into a hearty laugh, enjoying the inside joke because we both knew that Sheru had done that and would do it again.

The concept of "friend" was an intellectual conceit to Sheru.

He and I had had many debates -- drunken debates, about friendship and the meaning of friendship. He was passionate about it and I was rational about it.

Until one fateful night, when a man he had considered to be his closest and only friend betrayed him.

That man was me.

TONY and I had been recruited from the general populace based on our skill sets, while Sheru had entered RAW through the regular route, from the Indian Police Service (IPS) cadre. With his outgoing personality and being in the same core team during training, the three of us had bonded and become good friends.

Sheru liked me, finding me to be a perfect foil to his personality. Where he was cautious, I was daring. Where I was impulsive, he was strategic.

Sheru's childhood had been shaped by his small town upbringing, centered around a sugar factory where his father worked as a Boiler Operator. He was educated in a small school in that town. His father, desiring more for his only son, sent Sheru to Hyderabad for better education.

Unfortunately, the move backfired, and Sheru quickly connected with questionable company. He stopped attending school and started gambling using the money his father sent for the school fees. Sheru's uncle and aunt, his guardians, tried to warn his father, but he ignored their concerns.

When his father died, Sheru went berserk and dared the world to kill him. But the world spared him, and he slowly stabilized under the care of a local crime lord. This crime lord sent Sheru back to school, and groomed him to enter the police force. This was the foundation of Sheru's entry into the world of law enforcement, sponsored by his criminal godfather. Sheru quickly realized that the Indian Police Service was small fry compared to the intelligence agencies with their broad powers and deep pockets. He decided to join RAW with the express intention of using that access to grow his godfather's criminal organization internationally.

RAW was a place he could not buy his way into, so he used all the connections he could to make his entry and ascent rapid.

Priyanka entered our lives before I knew about this duplicity of Sheru's life. We both fell hard for Priyanka when she joined the RAW team as a junior RO. Priyanka chose me, and Sheru became insanely jealous. Our friendship became strained as Sheru maneuvered to get me posted elsewhere so he could pursue Priyanka.

It was then that Priyanka revealed to me Sheru's connection to the underworld. I decided to expose him, knowing fully well he'd be kicked out of RAW. My feelings for Priyanka and Sheru's aggressive efforts to pursue her attentions had something to do with it, I'm sure.

I approached the Chief with the information, and remember the last interaction between Sheru and me. He stared silently at me, and it looked like he could see deep into my soul. He said just one thing to me, "Don't trust that bitch." He meant Priyanka. He stepped into a waiting BMW with his Godfather riding inside, and was gone.

I followed his exploits even as Priyanka and I got closer, and eventually married. Sheru became an internationally recognized criminal. He escaped several slam-dunk convictions, thanks to key witnesses mysteriously vanishing into thin air or turning hostile even under the threat of prison time for changing their testimony.

I dreaded the day when we'd run into each other again. When I did see him again, it was at the Chief Minister's daughter's wedding. I was working security, and he was standing next to the Chief Minister with his arm around him.

He grinned at me, walked over, put his arm on my shoulder and said, 'Marriage suits you!' I gave a half-smile. He left.

Priyanka made me swear that I'd never interact with him again.

Going to Sheru in these circumstances was inevitable. I had known immediately that if anyone knew what had happened to Priyanka, it'd be Sheru. I even suspected he might have been the one to kidnap her, although I doubted it. Sheru had left us alone and I had no reason to believe he was behind this. But he'd know who was.

"I'D NEVER KILL YOU," Sheru said.

"You'd have someone else do it," I countered.

His voice and eyes became ice cold as he responded – "my enemies get one betrayal before I kill them. My friends get two."

"I'm not here to discuss the past. I want to know who killed Priyanka. Do you know anything about it?"

"Of course," he said, and my heart stopped beating for a moment. Would it really be this easy? This simple? "Look within," he continued. "RAW killed Priyanka and Tony."

I was stunned. This wasn't what I had expected to hear. I started to laugh. Disinformation has to be very subtle, and it has to be something the recipient is sub-consciously inclined to believe is in the realm of possibility. If Sheru was playing a game, he had just lost. What he said made no sense to me.

"I don't have time for bullshit, Sheru," I snarled.

"And you are next," he continued in a calm tone.

I wondered if he was threatening me, and quickly dismissed that thought. If Sheru wanted me dead, I'd be dead already.

'I'm blowing an operation I have had under progress for many years by telling you this, but when they killed Priyanka..." he trailed off.

It was clear Sheru still had feelings for Priyanka. My wife. I didn't know how that made me feel. Queasy was a word that came to mind. But if he did have feelings for her, his information had to be coming from the same perspective that I had.

The truth may not be absolute, but it could be our truth.

Sheru continued, "I've had an agent on my payroll within RAW, and he recently stumbled upon a list of names. All of them, RAW agents in the field, and each of them was systematically being eliminated. Tony's name was the third last on the list. Priyanka's was next. Yours was the last."

What the fuck.

"Priyanka is not a RAW agent," I scoffed.

"Maybe she was on there because she was connected to you," Sheru shrugged. "My agent merely memorized the list, and it took research on our end to realize that it was a kill list. The only reason it caught my attention was because it contained your name."

"And Priyanka's," I pushed, trying to ignore the jealousy I felt welling up in me.

"And your wife, Priyanka. Yes."

If this was a peace offering from Sheru, I wanted to take it. Badly. But I realized I was in a vulnerable position, and Sheru was in a position where it'd have been profitable to make such an offering.

"Why did you wait to tell me until after she was killed?" I probed.

"I didn't realize the urgency. I was trying to protect my agent by not connecting the timing of the information with his access patterns."

My mind was whirring trying to compute the possible moles in RAW working for Sheru.

I gave up. There could be, and were likely, several.

I lived in a world of deception, and nothing was more important to me than trust. If I were constructing Dante's Inferno, I'd reserve the worst level of hell for those who betrayed trust.

"Priyanka is dead." I said bitterly. If one could hang their head in shame without actually lowering it, they would probably be doing exactly what Sheru was doing as he stared evenly at me.

"And now, it's time for revenge", he offered.

"How do you propose I do that?" I was interested.

Sheru responded ever so calmly. "Become bait. We catch the killer when he attempts to kill you. That should lead us to his employer."

"Sure." I responded with mock enthusiasm.

"Do this, or become another victim of this conspiracy."

Despite all my feelings and misgivings about Sheru and his motivations, I realized what he was saying made sense.

I had to put a structure around the obvious - the fact that I was a target - that'd help me either survive the attack, or find the killers. Ideally, both.

"What structure do you have in mind?" I asked.

"TS14," was his curt response.

TS14 was a technique we had learnt in our earliest years at RAW. It was quite basic, and that's what made it work best for such situations where not much was known.

In TS14 the bait was equipped with a bulletproof vest, which would not protect him or her against a headshot. That was a risk. But the main concept around this technique was that the bait would setup several of their environments for break in and entry. Their transport vehicle, their apartment, their office, and one or two social spots. They'd restrict their life to use those environments, and only those because they would have been setup to enable monitoring, capture, and disarm.

In my case, it'd be my apartment, my car, and a safehouse that was RAW-owned. Sheru wanted to add a dance club he owned as a social spot.

Going to a dance club a few days after my wife's death didn't make sense to me. But Sheru convinced me with the idea that he'd send out rumors of possible leads available at the club to justify my visits there, including setting up a "Leopard" - a man who'd be the party with these supposed leads. The Leopard would also be part of the TS14 effort.

I pushed away the voice within me that kept asking all sorts of questions.

When you are stuck on the Sargasso Sea, you take any gust of wind you can get.

Even if it leads you to your doom.

SEVEN

THE UNDEAD WIFE

MY SAILS CAUGHT a gust that afternoon. With the plan in place, I drove back to my apartment.

That phone rang. I pulled over to answer.

"I'm listening," I said, my voice thick with rage and hate.

"No doubt," came the response from a male voice that I now knew belonged to Goru. "You want to meet me. Come meet me then."

"Where and when?"

"Airport. Pick up the ticket to Bangalore on Jet Airways waiting for you and enter the departure area. Spend ten minutes there. Not a minute more. Proceed through security and get on the flight."

"Why Bangalore?" I asked, curious about this twist.

"TS14," Goru said before hanging up.

Damn. They knew so much. I could be killed in so many different ways. They'd be monitoring every single person who bought a ticket after this phone call was made, and would zone in on and shadow all of my possible allies.

'Dammit!' This time I said it out loud. Made me feel a bit better. I accepted that perhaps this was the best way. I'd make some headway. Even if it killed me.

BANGALORE AIRPORT.

The flight there was uneventful. Sheru had tried to get a hold of me, but I ignored the call, going radio silent and pissing off Sheru. But it also alerted him that the game was afoot. He'd put his Plan B into action. Sheru always had a Plan B and even a Plan C. He was one of the best agents RAW had ever had. Such is the irony of life.

I stepped out of the airport. The phone rang.

Goru was terse. "Take the ticket waiting for you at the airline counter and enter the departure lounge."

He hung up before I could say anything.

I made my way back into the departure lounge and positioned myself with my back to a wall, and a good view of the entire terminal stretching out beyond me. I figured I was being watched. I wanted to meet my watcher.

As I waited, I noticed a security guard coming down the steps, passing several passengers going up the escalators on either side of him. He was dressed in a camouflage uniform and carried himself like a trained professional.

Our eyes locked and we both knew - Predator and Prey.

Only time would tell who would end up as who. Without a second glance, he continued on his way.

I wanted to follow him, but was stopped by an overweight man, who had come up beside me and tapped me on the shoulder.

"Mr. Abhay Gandhi?" He asked.

I turned and saw a rotund, smiling face. His question was rhetorical. He was wearing a suit. His right hand was in his suit jacket pocket. I wondered what it was holding. I didn't have to wonder for long.

"I have a dart gun, aimed at you. The drug tipped needle that'll enter your body will render you unconscious within a fraction of a second. Please don't try anything." He said everything matter-of-factly.

I stood up and he guided me towards the restrooms. I had to make a move - once we reached those restrooms I was dead. I could feel it.

A Policeman walked out of the restroom. As he walked past, I stepped around him and shoved him into the fat man, who instinctively pulled the trigger on his dart gun.

The Policeman went down in a heap.

I moved fast, throwing a karate chop to the fat man's neck. While he recovered, I dragged the Policeman under the staircase. I couldn't afford attention.

The fat man was struggling for breath. I decided that I'd deny him breath.

This is where I was -- in this moment where I was killing him -- where his scream was still stuck in his throat -- when my phone rang.

THE FAT MAN had let go of me and gestured towards the phone. I pushed him away, held him at bay with the Glock and answered the phone.

I heard my wife, my dead wife, speak.

SHE GAVE ME INSTRUCTIONS. "Don't hurt him, Abhay, he's a friend. And the Policeman isn't dead. Just knocked out."

She could clearly see what I was doing, so I looked around.

There she was - standing around a corner watching us, holding a phone to her ear. She looked glorious.

My dead wife was alive. It should have made me delirious with happiness.

All I felt was that I had been taken for a ride, made a fool of, sucker punched -- pick your favorite.

I was very, very pissed off.

EIGHT
CINEMA, CINEMA

It's an oddball trait for an intelligence agent to love watching Bollywood tear-jerkers and actually cry.

It was a trait I kept hidden away. The odd Sunday when Priyanka would leave on her travels shopping for antiques, I would indulge this trait.

"Mother India" was the mother of all tearjerkers. This black and white classic would get me every time. Without fail.

After I was done, I'd feel lightheaded, and rejuvenated. I'd call up Tony and we'd visit our favorite "Chandni Bars." Oddball places where men would drink, while fully-clothed women would dance and cavort around them, encouraging them to drink more.

It was one such night, when after a night of tremendous drinking, I had confided my marital problems to Tony. He had listened patiently, never interrupting, never taking sides, and had simply given me a hug at the end, and told me everything was going to be alright. I believed him, because I wanted to. I had never expected to find someone like Priyanka, to have a shot at a normal life in my profession. What I hadn't reckoned on was that a normal life, did indeed, include the normal possibilities of unhappiness, marital strife and yes, separation and divorce.

I had tried since to reconnect with Priyanka. I offered to accompany her on her antique shopping trips and she flatly refused, with a cruel jibe that she "preferred to have fun."

The day before she was kidnapped, she and I had had a huge fight over which TV channel to watch, leading to the question of whether we spend time together or watch TV separately, and in the end, slept in different rooms. Which is why the next day, I had spent the evening with Tony, leaving her alone.

Leaving her unprotected.

The guilt rose up in me, eating up my insides.

I thought I had lost her that night, and now, here she was.

Hale and hearty. And looking so beautiful, it hurt.

I wanted to run up and kiss her and never let her go.

All I did instead was fume.

Why hadn't she called me to tell me she was alive? Why did she let me think she was dead? Was this her way of getting out of this marriage? Perhaps she thought I'd ruin her life if she left me. I would never do that. But my mind desperately searched for motivations and came up with none.

She finally walked out from behind the corner and approached me. A tentative smile on her face.

"Abhay..."

I stood there silently, looking at a ghost.

"Abhay...", she said again, breaking into a run to hug me tight.

Out of the corner of my eye, I watched the fat man I had almost killed stand up, recover his breath.

I shoved my Glock down in my concealed holster as a couple of CISF guards walked by, eyeing us locked in a hug with a mixture of curiosity and amusement, and perhaps joy at seeing an expression of love in this place of comings and goings.

If only they knew that the love between Priyanka and I had withered away.

"I thought you were dead, but you are alive" said I, the king-of-obvious.

"You sound disappointed," came back the response. Never missing a chance to jab at my soul.

Here we go again, I thought.

Another fight, within a minute of meeting after her return from the dead.

We should divorce before we died, or the afterlife would be a long haul of marital turmoil. Who knew if divorce processes existed in the afterlife?

What if you are locked into the relationships of this world in the afterlife? My mind went through a set of ridiculous thoughts.

I watched the fat man finish a phone call and walk over.

"We must go. They must be watching you, and now they know you are alive," he said to Priyanka. She nodded.

I found myself being herded by them towards the exit. I didn't resist. The fat man pulled out an ID card and the CISF guards checked it, and to my surprise, saluted the fat man.

We left the lounge and headed to the passenger pickup area.

The fat man led us to a waiting Maruti Suzuki car, with darkened windows.

Dead giveaway the fat man belonged to some intelligence or police bureau.

Maruti is the most inconspicuous car in India, but one with darkened windows? Who does that?

As the driver pulled away, the fat man in the passenger seat and us in the back, I could tell the car's humble exterior belied the fact it had a custom-built souped-up engine.

"He saved me," Priyanka finally spoke, nodding in the fat man's direction, who turned around with a smile and a nod.

"Who are you?" I was tired of thinking of him as "fat man" which is totally not politically correct.

"Thyagaraja. CBI." He didn't hold out his hand, using it instead to rub his neck. "Priyanka," he continued, "you almost let your husband kill me back there, *yaar*!"

"*Yaar*" in Hindi has "pal" as the closest English equivalent.

I didn't know what to make of this pally relationship my wife had with a CBI officer.

"You two know each other?" I could sense the edge of an irrational jealousy creeping into my voice and I tried to hide it behind a broad smile. Priyanka saw right through all that.

"Listen Abhay, Thyagaraja was in the middle of a drug related raid, and they stumbled upon me being held by the kidnappers."

"Did you get any of them, Thyagaraja?" I asked the CBI officer.

"Please call me Raja," he responded. "Yes. Except for their leader. Very fair chap. He was the one calling you with instructions."

"Get that bastard!" I almost smashed Raja with my words.

"Of course, we have him now. We were just waiting to contact you first. He's in our custody and being taken to an interrogation site."

Goru! They had Goru. I was beginning to like Raja.

"Thanks for saving my wife's life, *yaar*," I said, and patted him on his fat arm.

"No problem, *yaar*. It's what we do." He responded with a happy laugh.

We were all becoming good pals here, I thought. So good, that if this was a Bollywood film, we'd break out in a song and dance about our *yaarana*, a friendship that lasted a lifetime and beyond.

I looked over at Priyanka. She reached out to me and held my hand.

The electricity surged through my body, triggered by her very touch.

For a couple whose marriage was shaky, I was always amazed how she had this power over me.

She smiled, her eyes twinkling with that magic I remembered from that summer day five years ago to the day. I smiled back.

"You okay?" I asked her, my voice the softest it has been in a long time. She nodded yes.

"I wanted them to call you and tell you immediately but..." she began, and trailed off.

"We didn't want anyone to know she was alive because we didn't know how much danger she was in..." Raja offered.

"I'm glad you are ok, that's all that matters." I interjected. "It might be best if we don't reveal you are alive." It felt odd saying that.

"It's too late for that. I'm sure they know by now that she's not dead," Raja said. "I wanted her to stay out of the action, but she insisted on being here when you arrived. She's a hard one to argue with," Raja laughed.

He had no idea what he was talking about.

Priyanka was impossible to argue with.

NINE
CHIT-CHAT OVER CHAI

In India, no occasion was inappropriate for chai. The arrival of a newborn, an auspicious wedding, or the death of an elder, chai was served everywhere, anytime.

I offered Goru chai at the start of our interrogation session.

Goru said nothing at all in response to my generous offer of chai.

I sighed. This one was going to be difficult. I took a sip of the chai I had offered him and made an appreciative sound, hoping that'd make him regret his rejection, but he sat across me, expressionless, restrained to his chair.

Well, he was soon going learn to have a productive conversation without the benefit of chai.

An interrogation was a physical battle between two individuals, and also a mental battle. We both knew the ride we were in for, and the jostling of anticipation, expectation and in our case, machismo, was a heady mix.

You're probably thinking I'm an asshole. Sure, I am. Who else is going to do this dirty work? Rich people get others to clean their homes, their toilets. You all want me to do this, because you'd never do it yourself.

This man had kidnapped my wife. This man had killed Tony. This man was out to kill me.

Those were the facts. I didn't know the whys, and the whos.

I had a job to do. I needed names and locations of the plotters. The ones who were pulling the strings.

"Needs more sugar," I made a face at the diminutive cup of chai. "Good thing you didn't drink it. It's not good at all."

I snapped my fingers. A junior agent took the cup and carried it away avoiding eye contact with both of us. Good, I thought. This agent has promise. Being able to resist the normal human impulses of curiosity were important qualities for a good agent.

They aren't kidding around when they say curiosity killed the cat.

I waited for the door to snap shut. Then, the buzz, indicating that the alarm systems were turned on. The chamber was now armed. The door could now only be opened from the outside after the alarm was turned off. If the door was opened from the inside the building would go into lockdown.

The ride had begun.

"Are you Parsi?" I asked him, as I stroked his fair face.

I was not expecting any response, but I saw him smirk. Good! He had fallen for one of the basic tricks an intelligence agent has at his or her disposal.

His opponent's own ego. I knew he wasn't Parsi, but by suggesting it, I made him relax, made him think I was stupid.

That alone would have been a win, but the fact that he smirked, that he let me recognize his internal thought process was colossal.

I didn't let on I had noticed by pretending to clean my nails.

"Answer me!" I yelled. I slammed my fists on the table fully embracing the roleplay of a dumb agent. I had an advantage in that Goru had managed to escape me at the fireworks market and therefore had a low opinion my capabilities.

I did not belong in his pantheon of heroes. It'd be easy to build on that.

I circled around the table. Stood behind him. Out of his sight. Watching his shoulders for a flinch, anything to show me that his body was scared of what could come next. Nothing. Goru was solid. He had no fear.

Huge ego. No fear.

I was confident this guy would never reach his thirties. And that was just fine with me. The good die young, they say. What they don't say is that the bad die young too.

I raised my arms. The air swished as they came down and smashed into either side of his head.

That had to hurt.

But looking at Goru's flushed, but calm, face, you'd think it hadn't at all. A slight flush when your temples had been slammed with a force of twenty kilos per centimeter is not a regular human reaction.

Goru was trained to handle torture. Which brought into question my earlier assumptions about his ego and his fear. Was Goru playing me? Followed quickly by -- was I getting paranoid?

I broke into a smile. Goru was a worthy opponent.

The game was afoot.

Prey and Predator circled each other, exchanging roles many, many times during that night.

I'll spare you the details but it was twenty hours later that I emerged from the room.

Exhausted, tired, torturing and tortured.

But I got what I wanted. A productive conversation with Guru.

Goru was a freelance assassin with a kill list he had gotten from an unknown client. His fee was deposited in a Swiss bank account. Damn those goddamn Swiss! That nation needed to be torn apart to give teeth to that old adage - 'crime does not pay.' Right now, it was certainly paying the Swiss abundantly.

Goru also revealed that I had been next on that kill list.

Tony had not been the first kill. There were others who had been killed in the past three weeks. Four to be precise.

With Tony and myself, that made six.

One of the other targets was Sheru. But the last one was unknown, making for a total of eight.

Goru wasn't lying when he said he would have been given his eight target only after he had successfully eliminated the first seven. Naturally, I didn't believe him and continued the torture. As a consolation for truly not knowing, Goru spilled the beans on Sheru - that he was in fact a RAW agent!

Sheru's whole persona was constructed to support his undercover work for RAW. But recently, Sheru had been turned by the General Intelligence Presidency, or the GIP, the intelligence agency of the Kingdom of Saudi Arabia.

They were now his true masters, and RAW had no clue about this.

My head spun with these revelations.

So Sheru was climbing the criminal enterprise success ladder but that was just a cover for being an undercover RAW agent, and then, somehow, he had been turned and became a double agent for the GIP.

I needed to warn Jacob.

I left a short casual message with a distress code on his voicemail. I knew that'd put him on alert and he would come meet me that evening at our designated spot.

I then did what any self-respecting Intelligence agent would then do in this situation.

I went to the restroom, sat down on the toilet and took a nice, long dump.

I never felt more shitty.

TEN
THE HANDLER

I WOKE up with a plan bouncing around in my head.

"Determine what was common among the agents targeted."

That was it. That was the plan. It'd be difficult given the federated nature of our organization, but I knew Jacob could help me.

I met Jacob a year after my induction into RAW. When my handler died of a massive heart attack, Jacob proposed himself for the job. Jacob wanted to get out of field work. He had trained to be a handler, and had shadowed several handlers, including mine, to prepare for the transition.

I was Jacob's first 'boy' in the field. Being called a 'boy' was a vestige of India's colonized identity. RAW was formed with the CIA's assistance in 1968, but the on-ground culture still reeked of British anachronisms.

Jacob handled my first real mission where I scored a 'notch' with my first kill.

The mission was to bring in an informer who had been turned.

When I arrived at informer's apartment, I found the door unlocked. I stepped inside and found him dead. His throat slashed.

My instincts fired up just in time to save me from the knife blow from behind that would have killed me. Instead, my assailant ran into my fist before running into the bullets from my gun.

I emptied the entire magazine into him.

My first kill.

My hands shook for a long time after. I had killed a human being.

Perhaps for some, killing came easy. I never had that luck.

Jacob took me out for drinks that evening. We spoke about a lot of things, none of which I now remember. I remember Jacob telling me for the first time the stock phrase he used with all his agents.

"You have a problem? I have a problem. We are family, Abhay."

Family. In some ways, Jacob was the only family I had left right now.

I met Jacob at a coffeeshop in Bandra. The specific distress code I left on his message triggered him to cut off all communications with the world and meet me at this coffeeshop.

He was waiting when I walked in. I got myself a coffee and a samosa.

"Hey," I said, sitting down at the table. "Want a samosa?"

Jacob nodded no. He wanted to know what was up. I could see that in his eyes.

But I took a big bite of the samosa and made a face showing how good it tasted.

Jacob scrunched up his face. "You dragged me away from my daughter's birthday party. You better have a good reason."

"Birthday party! Nice. How old is she?" I asked.

Jacob shook his head with more than a hint of frustration, but played along. "Six."

I sipped my coffee, wishing it were chai instead. "Nice age."

Jacob said nothing.

"There's a kill list. I'm on it." I broke the news. "Tony was on it. So's Sheru."

That got his attention.

"Goru is an American," I added.

Jacob shrugged. An American executing on a kill list of RAW agents. Goru would be in India for the rest of his life, rotting in Tihar as a play-mate of some powerful inmate. "Is he at our holding facility?"

"No. This is closed loop, Jacob. I don't know who to trust. There's a CBI officer involved. And…" I paused to make sure my voice wouldn't crack. "Priyanka is alive. Goru was holding her."

Jacob let that sink in. He nodded and patted my arm. Nothing more needed to be said about that. "Does he have a name?"

"Johnny Smith."

We both smiled. Getting this man's true identity would be an exercise in futility. He must have several passports. Each identity would culminate in a dead end.

"He shared this with me -- Sheru is undercover RAW, but, he's double-crossing us with the GIP. Have you heard anything about this?"

Jacob shakes his head gravely – 'no'.

I continued, "could Sheru still be loyal to RAW?"

Jacob shrugged, "your guess is as good as mine."

"How do we find out?" I prodded.

"We ask Sheru," he responded. "I'll arrange a meet," he said as he rose to leave.

Jacob, you win the award for the "Best Handler Ever", I thought, as he walked out the door, already on the phone making things happen with people who make things happen.

ELEVEN
THE TIGER'S LAIR

Lounge Parisien was close to Juhu beach. A fancy, upscale, invite-only bar in the basement of a commercial building. It came alive when the offices above shut down.

The lounge was open into the late hours, flouting all regulations. No one came to shut it down. All those in relevant positions of power received their monthly under-the-table fee for this privilege along with the occasional option to launder their ill-gotten gains.

Sheru was not involved in this bar, which made it a neutral and safer place to meet. The owner was highly motivated to ensure nothing happened on his property that'd attract the attention of the press.

Jacob and I arrived around noon.

We stepped into the elevator and three gunmen rode with us. Two levels up, the doors opened into a corridor that led to a security checkpoint. Everything and everyone was scanned. We had to surrender all our weapons, to be returned upon exit. These people took no chances.

In case someone with the intent to do damage made it this far, they would still not find VIP targets, because the arrivals were staggered. I expected Sheru to arrive a half-hour.

Sheru was, in fact, waiting for us in the lounge several floors above. He stood up as we entered.

"There's an assassin with a kill list, Sheru," I revealed watching closely for a reaction. The only reaction I could discern was one of surprise.

"Am I on it?" His tone laid-back, he grinned. "Am I?"

"You and I both." I replied.

"Who would want both of us dead?" His confusion was real.

I didn't know the answer. No one on one hand.

On the other, I suppose there would be various interconnections between our lives that may result in a list of many.

"Someone who has a goal in mind that either you or I or we both together can stop," I said.

"I don't see anything common between us, Abhay."

"Our work for intelligence agencies..."

"I quit RAW a long time ago..." he interrupted me.

"I wasn't talking about RAW. Not in your case" I interrupted him back.

He stared at me, searching to see how much I knew. I scoffed. And he knew then. He asked anyway.

"You know?"

I replied calmly, but there was a coldness in my tone. "About your loyalties to the GIP? Yes. I know."

"How did you find out?" he finally asked. "Ah. The American assassin told you." He answered his own question.

It was going to take me a while to think of my "Goru" as the "American Assassin." – but I had to.

"You face a treason charge when this comes out, Sheru," I said.

"It will never come out," he said. His voice had the edge of finality to it that comes to men who wield great power. His eyes penetrated my soul and not in any romantic way.

I realized that Sheru may not have killed me yet for betraying him once, but he'd certainly kill me before I got the chance to betray him a second time.

In that moment, I realized our weird non-friendship was truly done. Either I would kill Sheru, or he would kill me. But for now, we needed to work together to stay alive.

"Take me to him." Sheru demanded. We started retracing our steps out of this building and were soon driving in Sheru's sedan to meet the man who was hired to kill us.

Jacob chose to go back to his office. Field work was not his thing.

Sheru's sedan was bulletproof. But it also had armor plating built in that made it "bomb resistant," which is something I had no stomach to test out.

I suppose what it gave to all the occupants was a second chance at life in the event of an attack.

Sheru had to balance the drawbacks of visibility and vulnerability of this Sedan with the protection it offered. Most of the time, Sheru's men would have pre-cleared the path he would take. But this time we were going to a destination that was unplanned and off Sheru's usual routes.

We pulled up to the old house where Goru was being held.

The first hint of a problem was the fact that the gate was open and the guard was missing. Alerted, we pulled out our guns. The driver drove us inside. The guard lay prone on the ground in the middle of the driveway.

Sheru and I looked at each other. It had been a long time since our shared adventures at RAW, but it seemed like it was all just yesterday.

We easily slipped back into our operational mode.

Sheru's men stepped out, forming a protective cordon for us. We scanned for snipers. No one we could see.

We raced towards the entrance. The door was open. Sheru waved his men back. He knew we both had an equation and he didn't want his brutes messing up our rhythm. We stepped inside.

Sheru followed my lead, given I was familiar with the building. We reached the main room and saw the servant and cook, both unconscious on the sofa. They had been shot with the same darts I had used accidentally on that poor policeman at the airport.

Question was who had done it? The more urgent question was where was Goru?

Sheru took the left side of the house and I took the right. Saving the middle for after we had cleared out the flanks.

I crept into the living room, Glock held two-fisted in front of my chest, close, so it couldn't be knocked out of my arms.

The room had a large, with garish red fabric, ornate wooden sofa. Two side chairs sat on either side. Books were piled up on the coffee table. Bookshelves lined the walls.

I stayed close to the walls as I quickly scanned the room, and moved into the formal dining room.

Going down on my knees, I first checked under the table. Childish, I know, but I wasn't about to take a chance on the assailant being mature and too classy for the old under-the-table trick.

I moved towards the hallway area, expecting to see Sheru on the other side of the hallway.

I suppose that's why I released the tension a bit. Didn't want to accidentally kill Sheru and do the assassin's work for him.

I turned the corner, and saw Sheru, his gun in front of him staring in my direction. For a moment, I had the crazy thought that Sheru was about to kill me. He had that dull look in his eyes. Sheru's knees buckled. As he fell, he pulled the trigger.

The gunshot resounded through the house. Hitting the ceiling impotently. I turned, realizing Sheru's target was behind me.

But it was too late.

I felt the prick in my lower back. I looked down and saw a feathered dart sticking out, the red color of its tail clashed with the blue shirt I was wearing. I saw the black leather shoes of the assailant as he or she walked right up to my face and kneeled down.

Strange that my drugged brain would focus on fashion at a time like this.

The last thing I remember before everything went black was the assailant holding my arm to check if I still had a pulse.

I sure hoped I did.

TWELVE
THE BLACK AND SILENT

WHEN YOU SLEEP, you dream and even remember some of them. Sometimes those dreams continue throughout your life creating a parallel universe of characters and events with discontinuous coherence.

But being unconscious is a different thing entirely.

You are alive and you aren't aware of it.

People can cut you open and you'd never know it.

Who knew what happened on some deep internal level at the very moment of death? Maybe you become aware of everything despite whatever's happening to the body.

No one knows to this day what a human being experiences when they die.

I thought again of that old saying that my grandmother once told me - the pain you feel when life leaves your body exceeds the pain caused by a thousand scorpion bites.

I had not felt that pain yet. That must mean I'm still alive.

When my brain transitioned out of the black and silent world of induced unconsciousness. My eyelids flickered open. Light invaded my eyeballs and attacked my retina. Neurons exploded in my brain as all my internal machinery started to kick into gear.

I was alive.

That was my single thought as my hand twitched, searching for my trusty Glock, only to find that my hand was restrained at the wrist by a cold, metallic band.

I was strapped to an operating table.

I wondered what had happened to Sheru. It was a safe bet that he was going through a similar experience. I tried to turn my head to search for him.

I must have gotten someone's attention with my efforts because I was soon surrounded by white coats and some green ones. I couldn't see faces, all of which were masked and floated in the dark beyond the large light that shone down on me.

A hand reached out and turned the knob on a feeder attached to a tube coming from a machine.

Anesthesia. I was going under again.

I hated the black and silent world.

Being dead was not going to be my favorite state of existence. The black and silent for all of eternity.

The thought made me nauseous. I never got around to throwing up, because that thought along with all others were snuffed out by the powerful anesthetic coursing through my body, finding its way to my central nervous system.

Black silence.

SUNLIGHT.

It's the heat that gives it away from other human-made light.

There's a deep connection we have with the sun and its light that supports life on this planet.

I was coming back from the blackness. My body rocked. I heard the roar of a motor.

I recognized the sounds. A boat cutting through water. I was on it.

Before I could consider the various options, strong arms lifted me up. My eyes flickered open.

Two bare-chested, lithe fishermen, in *lungis* -- muscular in the way that only people who do manual work can be -- carried me to the side of the boat.

They swung me like I was a baby -- in, out, in, and before I realized what was going on, they threw me overboard into the water.

The Arabian Sea water rarely goes below twenty degrees centigrade. But it felt like I had hit a block of ice.

My body proceeded to sink.

I felt an unusual surge of energy. Adrenaline! A shot at survival.

I kicked my legs furiously and swam back up to the surface of the water. I broke through and looked for the boat.

It was already a distant speck. Too far to make out anything.

I turned around and searched for Sheru, wondering if he had gotten the same treatment. I saw no one.

The shore was off in the distance, but not so far that I could not make it.

I headed towards it swimming freestyle, easy at first then picking up speed.

I had to get back to land. I had to find out what was going on. There was something not quite right about everything that had happened.

Was Priyanka still safe? Sheru! What had happened to him? Who was behind this?

The questions jostled in my head for attention. They were all important, but the ones that really mattered all had to do with Priyanka.

I was not a religious man. But as I swam to the shore, with my angel having given me a second chance at life and delayed my entrance to the black and silent, I prayed for the first time since I was a child.

I prayed for Priyanka's well-being.

THIRTEEN
CHAKRAVYUHA

THE ADRENALINE HAD RUN its course and my exhausted muscles ached in agony as I swam towards the distant shore. I sank, my arms giving out, and my feet touched the bottom. I walked forward, finally breaking the surface and gasping for air.

With great effort, I made it to the beach and collapsed as the waves washed over me. My thoughts shifted to Priyanka and I began crawling forward, grabbing clumps of sand. Just as a wave threatened to drown me, a pair of strong hands pulled me up.

I found myself face-to-face with Jacob, my savior. He had clearly been waiting for me with a search team. "I got a call," he explained, "a man told me I'd find you here." I asked him if it was Goru, the assassin, and he confirmed that it was.

"Why did he save me if his mission was to kill me?" I asked.

"Maybe he didn't get paid," Jacob shrugged, "I'm just glad you're alive."

"Priyanka?" He could hear the tension in my voice.

Jacob hesitated, and for a brief moment, I panicked and thought the worst.

He said, "I don't know. She wasn't in the safehouse."

"They must have taken her." I hoped they had taken her. At least it meant she was alive. "What happened to Sheru?"

"I don't know. Raja is gone too. I was hoping you could tell me." He replied. "We've been searching for you all for three days."

I stopped in my tracks. "Three days?"

"That's how long you've been gone."

Jacob shook his head. "Let's get you looked at. We'll figure out what to do next."

There was one thing I knew I had to do next. Get Priyanka back into my life for good. And this time, I was going to be the perfect husband.

"YOU WERE SUPPOSED to be off the case and you run around everywhere, and violence follows you like your pet dog!" RAW Chief Iyer stabbed his finger in my face as he bellowed in my face.

I was in no mood for this. But I knew the game. So I said nothing. Where lives are at stake, negotiations get in-your-face. This was a negotiation. Chief Iyer was demanding I back off. I was setting the stage to ask for a lot in return.

"You contact your handler! You contact me! You don't take this into your own hands!" Chief continued his tirade.

"You contact your handler! You contact me! Don't take matters into your own hands," Chief continued his outburst.

I had enough. I knew what I wanted and Chief was either going to give it to me or I was going to take it. "I can put you into custody until all this settles, Abhay," he threatened.

"What are you waiting for, Chief?" I replied, not backing down from his empty threats.

I knew that if he took me into custody, he'd face a revolt from the department, who all knew and liked Priyanka. No one would question a husband's right to try and save his wife.

Chief sighed, and I felt like I had won the argument. But I couldn't let my guard down. Chief was cunning.

He walked up to me, placed his hand on my shoulder, and said, "there's more here than you know, Abhay."

"Tell me what you know," I asked, eager for answers.

Chief brought up information on a screen about, including the red alert that stated he was a "suspected GIP agent."

"It seems you've heard about Sheru being a GIP agent?" Chief asked.

I nodded in confirmation. Chief leaned back in his chair, steepled his fingers, and rested his chin on them.

"Sheru was our agent, Abhay. He went undercover for us, infiltrating the GIP. He's been feeding us information ever since," Chief revealed, leaving me in shock.

I couldn't believe it.

Everything I thought was true was suddenly false. Sheru was not my enemy, not a criminal, but a colleague and a valuable asset for RAW. I was feeling small and insignificant.

"Chief, this was never personal. Priyanka was kidnapped, and Tony and I thought Sheru might have had something to do with it. Tony died, and I went to meet with Sheru because I was told he was a GIP agent," I explained.

"Who told you that?" Chief asked.

"The assassin with the kill list," I replied.

Chief thought for a moment. "So the assassin killed Tony, targeted you and Sheru, and kidnapped Priyanka. There must be something connecting all of you. What is it?"

I shrugged, unsure of the answer myself.

"And why kidnap Priyanka?" Chief pressed.

Jacob, who was standing quietly to the side, interjected. "Chief, we think they wanted to have some control over Abhay. They wanted to use him to get to Sheru, who was the real target here, and Abhay was just a means to that goal."

"But why take Abhay and then release him?" Chief turned on Jacob.

My turn. "Chief, unless you tell me what you know, I can't help you."

Chief sighed. "Listen Abhay, once I tell you, your focus must remain on this mission. You will have to let us find Priyanka."

"Sure, Chief," I lied easily. Chief knew, but there was nothing he could do about it. He needed me. I could tell that by now. Otherwise, he'd have said nothing.

"There's a fragment we received from Sheru. It's a plan that is already in motion", Chief said.

I waited for Chief to continue. He took a long time to speak again.

The room was still. Silent.

"There are apparently several RAW agents who've been compromised, Abhay. And they are all on a mission to kill the Prime Minister of India on New Year's Day."

Chief let that sink in before he continued. "We think this kill list has the list of agents that are supposed to be compromised. We believe that it is a RAW unit carrying out these killings as a pre-emptive strike to thwart this plan."

"It may also be a list of people who can stop the plan from being executed." I countered.

"Which is why we are talking, Abhay. Why I've shared this with you." Chief was much calmer now, and more friendly.

"You'll get access to any resource you need. Except for clearance to the Prime Minister's Office and to the PM himself."

"Eventually, Chief, I'll need to meet with the target, and scope the potential arena of attack."

"Your mission will be to find Sheru."

I nodded. Not the time to argue with Chief.

"Jacob will facilitate everything you need." Chief turned his attention back to the desk. I nodded and turned to leave. Jacob got up to follow me.

As we reached the door of the office, Chief called out again.

"Good luck, Abhay."

I turned back, nodded an acknowledgement, and left. Jacob followed me out.

I had the distinct feeling as I left Chief's office that I was entering a Chakravyuha, like Abhimanyu did, the brave warrior-son in the Indian Epic Mahabharata.

Abhimanyu was able to enter the Chakravyuha, but could not exit.

Not alive, anyway.

FOURTEEN
SIPPING IN SILENCE

MY FIRST PORT of call was Ismail, the chatterbox who served as my unwitting informant. Everyone knew Ismail talked. So no one gave him information, but everyone asked him questions. Sometimes, the questions they asked him were the answers I needed.

Sheru was my current conundrum. Asking Ismail about Sheru's whereabouts held significant risks. Either Sheru's gang would latch onto my trail, hoping to recover their missing boss, or Sheru's rivals would hunt me down, eager to locate their enemy for a final, lethal confrontation.

But I had a third outcome in mind. I wanted to attract the attention of GIP, hoping they'd want their star asset back. And they did. In style.

I was at my apartment. Every entrance monitored. But to my surprise, the GIP agent slipped in as a resident, likely leaving the original tenant unconscious and stripped of their ID in some grimy alleyway.

The second surprise was the agent herself. I respect women in this business, but it's rare for them to show up at my door. Especially ones who, with a flawless American accent and the guise of an old friend, could nearly fool me.

"Hi! Is Priyanka in?" She asked.

I gave her a blank stare, which seemed to unnerve her a bit. Good. I let her flounder for a moment before she recovered.

"I'm her friend from New York," she continued. "We went to FIT together. Fashion Institute? We go way back." She laughed.

Her laugh was intoxicating, designed to make men fall for her. Didn't do a thing for me. Her American accent was impeccable. I was taken in by it until I noticed her hands. They weren't the hands of someone who worked with fabric. They were the hands of a killer, smooth yet strong. Clearly a martial arts practitioner. Some ridiculously high degree black belt, I assumed.

I offered her a false smile.

"She's not at home, unfortunately", I responded.

"Is everything ok?" she asked, concern seeping into her expression.

"No, not exactly," I played along. "Priyanka has been kidnapped."

This woman should have been an actor. Every nuance of her expression was right on. Not a hair out of place. She dropped her jaw open, just the right amount. Her eyes revealed her horrified thoughts as she thought the right thoughts, no pretense, but completely and truthfully immersed in the moment as "Priyanka's friend".

"Listen, why don't you come in? I'm sorry I had to break it to you this way. Have a drink, and I'll fill you in."

"Oh my God, yes, I need a drink. Is she ok? Have you heard... was it for ransom?"

"I don't know yet. I'm waiting for a call from them."

"This is so horrible! Poor Priyanka, she's the sweetest." She groaned.

She walked in, subtly scanning the place. She was good, and certainly easy on the eyes.

"I'll have Whisky on the rocks," she said.

I poured a drink for her, one for myself, and turned around to find myself into the barrel of her handgun.

"Is that part of your fashion statement?" I quipped.

"Shut up. Where are the cameras? What's the response protocol?" She demanded.

"Relax sweetheart." I tried to rile her. "We are all alone here. You and I and a couple of drinks with some very good whisky in them. So why don't we drink first, worry about work later."

She smirked. "For a guy who just lost his wife, you don't seem very concerned. Was she just part of the cover for you?"

Ouch. That was low. I asked, "Who are you?"

"I'm the one holding the gun."

I laughed. "Tell me something I don't know."

I handed her the drink. She considered it for a moment, put her gun away, and accepted the glass. We moved to the sofa, maintaining our distance.

We sipped in silence.

"I love my wife." I defended myself.

"I don't care," she responded bluntly.

"It's just that we've been having some marital issues. Priyanka is quite the independent type. I wanted more... I don't know... togetherness."

"I really don't care."

I shrugged and we drank in silence. I knew she was watching me to see if I made any move out of the ordinary that'd trigger the backups positioned in the area to come dashing in. I didn't. I actually did not want anyone to interrupt us. I wanted to get to know this woman. She had access to information about Sheru and his contacts and activities for the past several years, that'd be invaluable in finding him.

"What do you care about?" I asked.

"Information."

"Don't we all?" I laughed. "What do you want to know?"

She asked me questions. I answered her truthfully, to the extent I could. The story she got was that Priyanka was kidnapped, presumably to force me to do something, and that I was the target of a kill list. I mentioned that other colleagues were also on that kill list, but didn't mention any names.

She asked me point-blank: "I want the names of people on that list."

"I'm all that's left. The only other person alive, last I knew, was Sheru, the gang lord of South Mumbai," I answered.

"I need to make sure. Turn around."

I shrugged, stood up, and did as she said. I turned around. But I had positioned myself to be able to see her in a reflection and I saw her stand up now, a syringe magically appearing in her hand. Hell no! I was not doing the black and silent thing again.

As she walked closer, I ducked down, slid down on the floor and did a sweep with my feet. I managed to connect and knock her off-balance, dislodging the syringe in her hand which fell on the ground and bounced around.

Cheap plastic syringe. I guess the GIP was behind the times. With all that money, I had at least figured on a dart gun. And was all vested up to make that a hard-to-execute move.

We were in the middle of hand-to-hand combat. She seemed to be a student of Bruce Lee's Jeet Kune Do. I was a freestyle martial artist. Between the two of us and our moves, we managed to break the coffee table, all the liquor bottles, two lamps, several photo frames and one of Priyanka's prized hummingbird paintings.

I finally managed to get her in a headlock.

"We can work together," I hissed. "I want to find Sheru and I know you are from GIP and have information that can help me find him."

I let her go.

"How want to trust you?" She scoffed.

"Don't. I just need to save my wife, and I don't think I can do that without finding Sheru. I find him, I find my wife."

"Okay," she said.

"What's your name?" I asked.

"Sita."

"That's an old-fashioned name."

"It's the only one you'll get."

We shook hands. And I had a partner named Sita in my quest to find Priyanka and a second chance to set my life right.

The first place she took me to was Chandni Bar, a dive bar ten kilometers south of our location. Apparently, this was a place Sheru used to frequent. It wasn't for the décor, ambience or the liquor (he brought his own), so it must have been for one of the dancers.

Sita told me the dancer's name: Chastity.

"Now that's fashionable. Bet she knows how to shake a leg," I commented, earning a glare from her.

FIFTEEN
CHANDNI BAR'S CHASTITY

I COULDN'T HELP but ponder the coincidence between the alias "Sita" and the dancer's name, "Chastity." Sita, wife of Lord Rama in the Indian epic, "The Ramayana", had to face questions around her chastity after having been abducted by the demon king Ravana.

Clearly, "Sita" was a chosen name, and it revealed her penchant for meaningful connections.

This insight would be useful down the line. I had to pay close attention to everything she said and did. Everything would somehow be a connection to her core. Once I had a grasp on her core, she would become predictable.

We drove in her Hyundai. I could tell it wasn't modded. It must have been fresh from the showroom, a blank slate to avoid tracing any history an older car might carry.

The late evening traffic was a nightmare. We navigated through it. Sita drove like a seasoned pro. Navigating traffic in India is like threading through an intersection of aggressive fish schools, all dodging the shark. Constant vigilance was key—you could cause an accident if your attention wavered for even a moment.

Sita was focused and reserved. I refrained from small talk. I wanted her to speak freely without my prompting.

"I really did study fashion in New York," she said out of the blue. A bid to assert her integrity. Another glimpse into her psyche. A point I could use against her.

"I believe you," I responded.

"Your wife, she studied there too, you know."

I didn't. There was a lot about Priyanka I didn't know. My mind went back to that time.

I met Priyanka during a short trip I had made to the US six years ago. It was a random meeting in a bar I had gone to with my friends. The waiter had delivered her drinks to us, and she had come over to claim them. I liked her spunk. She liked... actually, I'm not sure what she liked about me. Perhaps it was just the fact that I was the only one who got my tongue untied fast enough to say that she couldn't take the drinks away, but she and her friends were welcome to join us. She made a face, grinned and called her friends over.

"You are not some rich wall-street types who believe every woman can be bought, are you?" Priyanka asked.

"Hell no," I said.

"Just our luck." She joked as her friends joined us.

Priyanka and I couldn't take our eyes off each other for the rest of the night. That was the first night we kissed. She didn't let me get any farther than that. I returned to India the next day. It took me three months to get brave enough and drunk enough to send her an email. She took three days to respond. Three days of hell for me where it got so bad that Jacob came to check up on me. I told him all, and he had laughed and laughed before breaking the terrifying news to me.

I was in love with Priyanka, he said.

I disagreed vehemently.

Three months later, Priyanka and I had gotten married in an Arya Samaj marriage ceremony. Her family, she said, was against the marriage and never had any contact with me, and cut off all ties with her. She came to India to live with me.

Things had been great for several years. Then, we started having difficulties. We become more distant. Disconnected. Last year, after a trip where she had gone to Kanyakumari, Priyanka had returned very disturbed. Everything I did seemed to bother her. She seemed to hate every single thing about me, more so than ever. I was convinced she had had an affair in Kanyakumari, or worse, she had been having an affair all along, and it had ended during this trip to Kanyakumari. There was no other explanation for this sudden change in her behavior. I thought about using my resources to, well, spy on her. But that was a road I was not willing to go on. I wanted our lives to be that of a typical married couple. With typical couple difficulties.

A loud honk brought me back to the present.

Sita braked hard to avoid hitting an errant taxi trying to cut in. She let him win the battle. Minutes later, we reached our destination.

Shanti Park, Mira Road, Mumbai.

There was no real parking near Chandni bar. We just found a spot on the side of the road, and left the car to its fate as the traffic bent around it using every single inch available.

Sita led the way. There was no sign on the building, and we climbed up several steps and entered through a set of curtains. Sita seemed quite comfortable walking into a bar where women were nothing more than exploited entities. I suppose she felt confident they'd never be able to bring her in here on those terms. Not with that gun she packed.

We walked into the place. A few heads turned. Understandable. Such a well-dressed woman walking into such a wretched place.

A female cashier looked up, a little surprised as Sita breezed past her and the bouncers. I followed. No one tried to stop us which surprised me a little.

Chandni Bar was a squarish room, four pillars in the middle carved out a smaller square where five women dressed in low-cut blouses and wearing skirts danced to loud Bollywood music. Tables encircled them, occupied by men in various states of drunkenness. The clientele was mixed, with several tables occupied by groups in suits.

Sita moved past the tables to the far side of the room. She reached a door. A bearded man, wearing a skullcap, stood up, but didn't stop Sita as she kicked the door open and walked into the room. I walked in behind her, a wave of admiration flowing through me for this woman!

The room was clearly a manager's corner. I guessed the man on the phone, with his back to us, and his feet up on a shelf behind the desk was the guy in charge of daily operations. He had his hand out and was waving us out of the room without even a look at us. Sita stood in front of him, her arms folded. I walked up to the table and hung up the phone.

"Hello?" the manager turned around to see me with my hand on the phone cradle. "Who the hell are you, bastard?" he added.

Friendly asshole, I thought. But I felt introductions were in order. "Abhay", I replied. "And that's Sita."

He turned to look at Sita, and burst out into laughter. "Chastity! You bitch! Where did you run off to? Huh? Sheru may be gone, but you still work here."

Sita was Chastity! Chastity was Sita. I suppressed a grin as Sita/Chastity flashed a look of "gotcha" at me. Clearly, she was undercover here as a bar girl, and Sheru had not done anything to really change that impression the manager had. I had a feeling that Sita might approach it differently now.

"Where did you get those fancy clothes? Huh? Take them off! Go get in your work clothes. My clients don't want some high-class bimbo, they want someone on their own level." The manager turned his attention to me. "Abhay, huh? How about I light your ass on fire, then you will feel fear. Who are you? Police? Get the hell out. She is my girl. Nothing you can do here. Go on, out!" He yelled out for his guy, "Mohammed!"

The man with the skull cap entered the room, running straight into my fist. He fell to the floor like a bag of flour. The manager was on his feet. "You bastard!" He yelled. "You will regret that, you son of a whore!"

He came around the table, intending to do me harm, I'm sure. But I never got a chance to find out. Sita/Chastity grabbed him by shirt and slammed his face into the wall in a very cool Judo move. I decided there and then that I wasn't ever going to pick a fight with this woman. Never ever.

The manager came to. The shock on his face was complete. If this hadn't convinced him he was playing outside his league, the Colt that had magically appeared in Sita's hand certainly did. "Don't kill me," he pleaded. "What do you want?"

"Where is Sheru?" Sita asked.

"I don't know..." he never got to finish that sentence as Sita's Colt slammed into the side of his face. I worried that he was going to fall unconscious and we'd have to hang around until he came to, not an option I cherished. But that didn't happen. The manager seemed to have a thick head. "There's a man..." he said, wanting to make it clear he was giving information we wanted. "He can tell you."

"Which man?"

"Abdul", the manager said. "He works in Colaba. Ask for Abdul Mechanic... anyone will know."

"Pay the girls double today. Or I'll come back."

The Manager found that option painful, so nodded eagerly, impatient to get rid of us. He was not a gang leader, just a dispensable cog-in-the-wheel, and as such, he really didn't have the freedom to stir up trouble. Or take initiative. That money would have to come out of his pocket, but it was a small price to pay to avoid a Colt whipping.

We got up just as Mohammed was coming to. He saw his bloodied boss on the floor sitting across from him, and made no trouble for us. He hurriedly got up, opened the door for us politely, nodded a friendly goodbye, and shut it quietly behind us.

Nice guy.

SIXTEEN
ABDUL: THE FIXER OF BROKEN THINGS

CLANG!

The sound of metal hitting metal rang out—sharp, rhythmic. We walked up a small alley, easily finding folks who knew Abdul, the Mechanic.

Mumbai, transient yet steady with a large, long-standing population. Communities where everyone seemed to know everybody—or at least someone important like Abdul.

Abdul, a mechanic in craft but much more in spirit—a confidant, philosopher, advisor, peacemaker, fixing more than just vehicles.

We found him under a Premier Padmini, hammering out a dent above the right rear wheel.

"Abdul Chacha, visitors," called an assistant, who'd led us the last bit. Chacha, a term for an elder or uncle.

The banging ceased. "Ha?" Abdul called out.

"Visitors, chacha," the young man repeated, louder, then walked away, head shaking.

Abdul didn't hear so well, I guessed.

Abdul pushed himself out from under the car and sat up. He was a young man, perhaps in his early thirties. Handsome. I could see him being a socialite in another life. He sat there, and wiped his dirty hands on an even dirtier piece of cloth before he looked up and saw us. He recognized Sita instantly.

"Chastity madam! Welcome, welcome!" he broke out into a smile and yelled out to his assistant. "Yunus! Chai!"

"No Chai, Abdul." Sita said. "I'm here for information."

"Over chai. Everything we discuss over chai." Abdul was a charmer. I could see that easy enough. He looked at me a couple of times, sizing me up, then decided to ignore me. Sita owned the power ball here. I didn't mind. Staying in the background allowed me to observe more. Like that assistant, who brought us the chai, then retreated and prepped an AK-47 trying to keep a very low profile, and followed us from a distance.

Given Abdul's image as a confidant and peacemaker, a man wielding an AK-47 was not a good sign. There was someone here waiting for some-one, and it was a good chance it was us they were waiting for. I tried to catch Sita's attention, but she was busy being charmed by Abdul.

It happened very fast. The message and the visual must have gotten to the decision makers and the chai man arrived. He held out the tray with the small glasses half-filled with light brown chai. Sita took a glass off the tray. I was desperately searching for the source of danger that made my spine tingle in terror. Then I saw him. Just a glint in a second story window across the street.

I reached out to the tray, and instead of the glass, I grabbed the chaiwala and turned him to face the window giving myself a shield. With my other hand, I unholstered my Glock and aimed at the assistant behind and to the right, raising his AK-47. I fired. The shot hit the assistant in his face. He went down.

Sita was moving too. She grabbed Abdul and pushed him towards the direction we had come from. The sniper on the second floor window fired hitting the poor chaiwala. He died instantly. Sita and I both fired at the window and the sniper ducked out of sight. I dropped the chaiwala's lifeless body to the ground and covered Sita from the back and she pushed Abdul in front of her and we made our way to our car.

"We can't go back to the car." I shouted. Sita was on the ball. She was already turning into a sidestreet. There was an Autorickshaw parked, the driver enjoying a smoke. We ran towards it. "Move or die, Abdul, your choice!" Sita yelled at Abdul who was trying to slow us down. He chose to move.

We reached the auto, and I pointed my gun at the autorickshaw driver who just shook his head. "Steal a nice Mercedez, saab! Why do you want to take my auto?"

"Get out!" I yelled. Cursing under his breath, the driver got out and took the driver's seat. Abdul and Sita slid into the backseat. I turned the key, and the auto started up. "Don't worry, I'll leave your auto three blocks away." I comforted the driver as we pulled away.

Gunshots echoed out behind us. Dammit! If any of them hit the gas cylinder that provided power to this, we would explode. People were scattering and that helped us take a right turn into another street that got us out of the gunfire. Then, it was a race to reach the main street, where we quickly melted into the traffic.

"I didn't have anything to do with this," Abdul pleaded. "They made me do it."

"They who?" Sita demanded.

"Sheru's men." He answered.

I took another left off the main street and pulled to a stop under a tree. Traffic continued to whiz by us. I got out and went to the rear seat. I grabbed Abdul by his hair, and punched him square in the face.

"Don't lie. Sheru's men would want us alive. Who were they?"

"I don't know. I really don't."

"You know, Abdul. That's your business. Where's Sheru?" I switched to the more important question.

"He's been shot, but he's alive. That's all I know. He's in some place with doctors. That's all I heard. He was found with some woman who saved his life."

I smiled. Priyanka. It had to be. Now all we had to do was find out where Sheru was. And I'd soon have my Priyanka back.

As for Abdul, we weren't done with him yet.

"You are taking us to Sheru." I got back in the auto.

"But I don't know..." Abdul protested.

"We'll keep driving around until you find out." I responded.

Abdul may not have the information we wanted, but he sure had the means to get it for us.

The auto pulled back into traffic. We needed to get a better ride.

It was time to call Jacob.

SEVENTEEN
PRIME MINISTER'S OFFICE

Jacob was at the PMO when I called, his tone hushed. He was in the anteroom at the PMO building with the Chief waiting for the Prime Minister to arrive.

"Any leads?" He asked. I could feel the pressure in his voice. He was under the gun, as I'm sure, was Chief. It was unthinkable that there was a plot to assassinate the PM that involved a RAW agent.

But India was not new to a member of the security apparatus being responsible for the death of the country's leader. Indira Gandhi, India's fifth PM has been assassinated by her own two Sikh bodyguards. She had insisted on keeping them despite advice to the contrary, after she had approved the use of force at the Golden Temple, a place sacred to the Sikhs. Proving that the most effective way to turn a man was by using faith and God. Money only goes so far.

"Nothing PM-worthy." I said, feeling his disappointment in the ensuing silence.

"Anything you find, call me." Jacob urged, his desperation clear. Our organization was under attack from the inside. If this plot succeeded, RAW would cease to exist.

"Jacob, I need a pocket," I said to him.

Pocket was what we called a pool of cash, set of bank accounts and credit cards that acted as our petty cash account for off-the-books or unpredictable missions. There was rarely any oversight or accounting for the money in these "pockets", and it'd be a lie to say they were always used for a mission. Then again, our definition of a mission was vague. Who knew what connection would help us when. So we always made connections. Knowing some would pay off, and others would never amount to much.

"Ramesh will get you sorted," Jacob replied, then hung up abruptly as the PM arrived.

I returned to the commandeered cab which had replaced the auto rickshaw. The driver was no in the passenger seat, scared out of his wits. Abdul and Sita were in the back.

"We need to get to the state bank, it's three kilometers away. Give or take." I told Sita.

"Bank robbers?" The scared cabbie had found his voice. "Please don't involve me. I have a wife, three kids! I'll get out here, I won't tell anyone..."

"Shut up!" I drawled. I wasn't sure if it was my voice or Sita's Glock that took aim at him that did the trick, but the man shut up.

"Abdul's not being very talkative." Sita said.

"He just needs some motivation. Right, Abdul?" I turned to him. My eyes had gone cold. The stakes were too high for this idiot to play games with me. My Glock was out before anyone could say "Abhay", and --

BLAM!

Abdul's scream mixed with the cries of the Driver. Abdul's shattered kneecap had splattered in the car. With a grimace, I wiped a piece of it off my face.

I turned back and aimed the gun at the driver, whose screams died before they were even a thought in his brain.

"Warn me next time!" Sita snapped.

"And spoil the surprise?" I quipped. "Abdul's going to be as talkative as you want now."

I turned back to the steering wheel, and started the car. We pulled away from the curb, where a few passersby stuck in that place between being scared and curious were walking away from the car after hearing the gunshot, even as they keep trying to see what was going to happen next.

Within moments, we were moving, and I tuned out Abdul's screams and focused instead on the unfolding narrative.

Priyanka's abduction, Tony's death, Sheru's disappearance, and now, the assassination plot against the PM.

The priority was clear: find Priyanka, save her, and reclaim my life. The exposed plot would surely tighten the PM's security.

Abdul's screams entered my consciousness again. They weren't just screams now. He was trying to form some words. He was trying to say the name of a place. It was a place I was very familiar with. It was the place where Sheru and I had hidden out after a mission to cool off. It was safehouse that had now become a mob house. It made sense that Sheru would be holed up there.

Abdul screamed again. His words still unintelligible to Sita.

"Sector 20," I said, to help out Abdul.

"Do you know where it is?" she asked.

I nodded. I knew exactly where in Navi Mumbai we had to go to get to Sector 20, and who to ask for Sheru's exact location.

But I wouldn't need to ask anyone. Sheru had arranged for a reception committee.

EIGHTEEN
BULLETS OVER NAVI MUMBAI

LEAD. Piercing. Flesh. Shredding fibers. Hitting bone. Taking life.

Bullets—beautiful and violent, much like love, much like life itself.

Abdul was silent, staring into space. Likely in shock from his shattered knee. Poor bastard.

The drive to Navi Mumbai was straightforward, albeit lengthy. I had an informant who could point us to Sheru's location. We arrived at his Kirana Store and parked. A black Maruti halted behind us. I didn't pay much attention to it as I walked around the front of my car towards the store. Two men exited the Maruti. Both looked like average Joe's, or I suppose, average Jai's, given this was in India. They headed to the store, falling in step behind me.

"Hey", one of them yelled out. "Abhay?"

I turned, expecting to be shot in the face. Right between the eyes. But I saw the men weren't holding any guns. Messengers. Or delivery men. I was safe for the moment.

"Yes?" I responded cautiously.

"Sheru wants to meet," they said. It seemed my luck hadn't run out yet.

"Abdul..." I started to say.

"We'll take care of him. You come with us."

Sita exited the car. "I'm coming too."

The men looked at each other, shrugged. As we walked to their Maruti, they took aim at Abdul and fired several times.

"We took care of him. Just like I promised." The man laughed. The other one looked at me without any expression. I grit my teeth. But there was nothing I could do. Abdul had broken the one rule a confidant had. Never tell the secrets you are given. These men had just made sure he'd carry the rest of them with him to heaven or hell, wherever he was headed.

As the Maruti drove past the cab, I saw Abdul's bloody face pressed against the window, his eyes wide open in terror. The poor bastard had tried to get out and run -- but you can't outrun death.

The men took us through narrow alleys that could never fit any car larger than a Maruti.

Streets that looked like dead ends, opened up when brick walls built on tracks were shoved aside to allow the Maruti to pass through. Men with AK-47s positioned on corners were part of the defenses we could see. Hidden snipers and a machine gun nest or two the part we couldn't.

We drove into an open area covered by a straw roof and surrounded by this rundown slum. A building in the center of the open area was was utilitarian and heavily guarded, with several openings in the walls that made it clear that this building was a bunker. A fortified machine gun nest. I was certain there were tunnels that'd allow the occupants to escape into the slum from where they'd disappear. But there was no chance any law enforcement would ever get this close.

I was an exception. I knew Sheru was counting on the fact that I'd never leave this place alive.

Sita and I had not talked on the ride here. Not one word. I suppose we were both going through our respective game plan. Our collaboration exercise would end once we got to Sheru, and now that we were within striking distance of achieving that objective, we were just lone wolves, each with our own mission. I figured she had a better chance of getting out of this one alive.

We stepped out of the car. I entered the structure with the two men who had brought us here while Sita was escorted by two other gunmen who took her to the far side of the structure.

"Akbar!" the silent one yelled out. Akbar, a teenager, probably fifteen ran up and gestured for me to raise my arms. I did, and he started to pat me down. Very thoroughly. He removed my handgun, my ammo clip, my handleless knife hidden inside the sole of my shoe. This boy found every single weapon I carried. He clearly knew his job and I felt violated.

The inside revealed a rich man's house in the middle of a dirt poor slum. Here, every detail was exquisite. Leather sofas, graceful lamps, indoor greenery, plush carpet, designer lighting, you name it. It was all tasteful perfection, right down to the designer doorhandles and knobs.

I was led into a room that had leather couch. I sat down. The men left me and shut the door on their way out. I didn't bother getting up and checking anything. I figured I was on a video camera and the longer I looked like a threat, the longer the delay before they felt it was safe to let Sheru in.

So I sat motionless on the sofa. They could watch me to eternity and I wouldn't flex a muscle.

Sheru walked in a couple of minutes later. He looked a sight. His head was shaven with two rows of fresh stitches. A bandage on his left arm. He was limping. His face haggard.

His Man Friday followed a few steps behind.

I said nothing. He sat down in front of me.

"Drink?"

Without waiting for my response, he motioned to his Man Friday who quickly returned with two glasses of Chivas Regal on the rocks. He placed them in front of us then exited the room.

"Priyanka. Is she alive?" I asked.

"Ask your people." He responded. "RAW is holding her."

"That's a lie."

"Is it?" He asked. "Who else knew where she was?"

"IB did. Raja might have talked to someone."

"Bullshit. They used Priyanka to drag you out. And then they used you to drag me out."

"Who's they?"

Sheru leaned forward. He always did this whenever he had something really important to say. "Whoever it is within RAW that's planning to assassinate the Prime Minister."

"Someone within RAW is planning to assassinate the Prime Minister?" I sniggered. "I know that you are a double agent for GIP -- "

"You know shit." Sheru cut me short. He pressed a button on the side of the table. The door opened and his Man Friday entered.

"Bring her in," he ordered. The man left to do his bidding and Sheru turned to me.

"The woman you came here with. Do you know who she is?" He asked. I shook my head no.

"She's an agent for GIP. They've been trying to recruit me for several years now. But they have failed."

"I don't believe you."

"She'll tell you herself."

"Why was she so interested in finding you?"

"Because it's their agent who discovered this plot. And they want to stop it. But the problem is their agent has disappeared with the info he had on this plot. She's hoping I could help her."

"Who were the people who kidnapped us? Why did they let you go?"

"RAW! It's those people who probably de-briefed us under drugs to make sure we knew nothing. They didn't let me go. They were going to kill me. My men rescued me. You on the other hand, you got a fighting chance. But they kept Priyanka, just in case you got close again."

The door opened again and Sita entered.

She had let her hair loose. She had her handgun with her. She slipped it into the holster in the small of her back as she walked up. She took a seat across from Sheru and sitting an arms length away from me. It was clear that it wasn't me she wanted to speak with. In fact, she barely acknowledged my presence.

"I need to speak with you, Sheru. In private." She said.

"Abhay is an old friend. I need to show you both something. Then, if you still want to talk..." Sita moved closer to him, grabbing his face with her hands and kissing him.

A passionate kiss. It took Sheru by surprise for a moment. I sat there. Uncomfortable. I was wrong about her being the one who was in danger.

"You were hard to find," she complained to him after pausing the kiss for a moment.

"A natural byproduct of being kidnapped and tortured. Yeah, I guess I felt pretty anti-social for a while...", he responded.

"Who did this to you?"

"I was hoping you could tell me." he said, a trace of accusation in his voice.

"We had nothing to do with this, Sheru. Believe me. I wanted to find out what had happened to you because we had learnt about the plot and wanted to stop it. That's all."

Sheru thought for a brief moment. "Well, tell me how you got that information, and I'll tell you what I know."

She smiled, smirked even. "I can't do that because I don't know. We have someone on the inside, and whoever it is, they don't want to be found. Everything is anonymous. We've tried to send information and payments, ciphered, trying to see if we could trace his or her identity via deposits, you know, all the usual tricks, but no luck. They don't want to be found, but we have reason to believe the plot is a real and is in play."

Sheru turned to me. "Chief told you about this plot?"

I kept my mouth shut. I had no desire to offer corroboration or any commentary on the fact that I and part of RAW knew about this plot too. I shrugged. "I'm here to find Priyanka," I replied.

Sheru got up, grimacing from pain. "Follow me."

Sita and I stood up. We exchanged a glance. A different dynamic in play now. She clearly was an insider to this world.

"Do I get my handgun back?" I asked.

"Not until you leave this place." Sheru replied. "For your own safety. Anyone here sees you with a gun, they'll shoot you first and ask questions later."

Sheru held the door open. Sita glanced at me. I must have been staring at her because Sheru pulled me aside and whispered in my ear -- "this one is mine."

And here we were again. Just like old times. Sheru and me, and a woman that we both were clearly attracted to.

Lucky for Sheru I was already married, even if unhappily so.

NINETEEN
SITA'S JUSTICE

SHERU LED us down a bright corridor, stopping at an apparent dead end. He pressed a hidden spot, revealing a high-tech security panel. After entering a code and scanning his thumb, the wall slid open to a new section.

Another secured door awaited, and with another code entered, Sheru ushered us into what resembled a war room—equipped with a large table, chairs, and multiple large screens, each with an iPad in front.

Sheru gestured for us to sit. As we did, the iPads lit up, and one of the wall monitors flickered to life. Sheru settled next to a touch panel, keyed in his password, and confirmed his identity with a thumbprint, revealing a custom user interface on the screen.

Some software company had made a ton of money building all this software. I had a sneaky suspicion that none of them lived long enough to enjoy it.

Sheru brought up a list of names on the screen. The kill list. I saw my name. Tony's. Sheru's was on there too.

"Sita sent this. It's a plan to eliminate RAW agents before hitting the

Prime Minister," Sheru began. "And the theory is that it's in preparation for assassinating the Prime Minister of India."

"Not a theory. It's an active mission." Sita corrected.

"Whose mission?" I probed.

"We don't know. India has a lot of enemies. Could be the Chinese. Pakistan is an obvious choice, but we doubt they'd go that far. It could be someone unrelated for some strategic or tactical benefit we don't yet know." She replied.

"Could be yours." I watched her carefully for her reaction.

"You wouldn't be sitting here alive if it was," came her swift, icy retort. I decided that underestimating Sita's resolve to take my life if her mission called for it, would be the last thing I did in this sad life of mine.

"A rogue ISI outfit?" I persisted.

"We have the ISI well-penetrated," she responded. "It's not them."

"And who's we?" I asked.

"Not your concern," Sheru interjected.

"She's GIP, isn't she?" I was going to be a pain in the ass if I had to.

"You can reach whatever conclusion you want to." Sita interjected.

"I need to know how accurate this information is, if you are expecting me to do anything about it."

"Who said you have to do anything about it?" Sita said.

"Isn't that why we are talking?" Now I was really unsure of what the objective was here.

"We are talking because we need to know who our mole is in RAW. We believe he knows the details of this plan but has gone radio silent as the plotters have gotten close to him." Sita said.

"Then we just track down all the foreign agents..." I began and was cut short by Sita.

"Not foreign agents. We believe the plotters are RAW agents. This is a plan within RAW." Sita said, watching me carefully as I had watched her only a few moments ago.

"What? That's ridiculous." I scoffed, but deep inside, my brain was already weighing the option. Trying it against all the facts to see if fit, or could fit.

Would RAW kill the PM if he was CIA's puppet?" she challenged.

I paused, stunned. Her claim was new to me.

"We have proof—deposits in his Swiss accounts..."

"This government's losing the next elections. Why act now?" I questioned.

"We believe there's a clandestine deal at play," she explained. "Perhaps a secret deal being worked out between India and the US that is not in India's best interest."

"Nothing of that scale could escape the press," I argued.

"Please, Abhay...", this was the first time Sita had addressed me by name, and I have to admit, it felt good. She continued. "Don't be naive. The press is up for sale in India. Promise them a few quarters of advertising that'll help them meet their corporate numbers and they'll do anything you want them to. The government won't directly buy up that advertising, but they have enough quid pro quo with business tycoons to make that happen easily enough. As for debate, that will not apply, if it's related to the intelligence communities. That falls directly and only under the Prime Minister."

I was starting to see a motive, however irrational it seemed. But the strategic value for the CIA to essentially have full access to RAW would help solve their dilemma in South Asia. They'd have intelligence on the ground that'd take them decades to develop and given China's meteoric rise, this was a golden opportunity for them. But could this even be possible? Before I could pose the question, Sita elaborated.

"This is not being driven by the CIA, but by a small cell within it. We were lucky enough to have a translator embedded in that group."

"A translator?" It was odd Sita would give away that specific bit of information.

"He was killed. Otherwise, I wouldn't mention it. But I know you need something to hang your coat on. Check on that. This plot is real. There's a group within RAW that handles corruption within India. It's been a splinter group that has very little oversight. We know very little about it. The targets are randomly generated by computer algorithms that correlated data to arrive at a list of plausible agents involved in that group."

"Sheru, Tony and I were involved in corruption-related cases."

"That's probably why your names ended up on the list." Sita nodded. She already knew. "Since Sheru had left RAW, they tortured him to determine if he really had. I guess you have."

I watched Sheru, knowing he was indeed with RAW.

"I told them nothing, one way or the other." he said.

"They must have used drugs." She said.

"Because there was nothing to tell. Drugs wouldn't have given them any information that was useful."

"You clearly aren't a member of that group." Sita said to me.

"I've been charged to uncover and destroy them." I finally revealed. It was clear that we were all friends here. What I had learnt was incredible, and the blocks had started coming together in my head.

"They are holding Priyanka so they have leverage over you, just in case you get too close." Sita said.

That made sense. But how would they contact me even if they ever wanted to communicate their demands to me? That cell phone was long gone. I didn't ask the question figuring that when they wanted to contact me, they'd find a way.

"I have to find her. I have to rescue Priyanka."

"Yes. She would have information about them by now that'd be very useful." Sita responded dispassionately.

I didn't much care for Sita's attitude towards saving my wife. But I was thankful to her for having given me a big piece of the puzzle. This was critical in understanding the scenario, in figuring out who was a friend, who was the enemy, for this situation. In my world, friends and enemies changed sides too often, and it was really an art to determine who was who in each situation you faced.

"But we have no leads." Sheru added.

"I can generate leads. I need to get out of here." I stood up. As I did, I pressed the top toe area of my left shoe. From the back, a small bug ejected itself and rolled under the sofa. No one noticed the small gap in the back heel as I moved forward. Sheru pressed a button to summon his Man Friday, and barked orders at him.

"He leaves now. Give him his gun back."

His Man Friday nodded and gestured for me to follow. Without a backwards glance, I left with him.

Moments later, my former two companions drove me out. This time I was blindfolded very effectively. When they finally removed the blindfold, almost an hour later, I had lost all sense of location. I stepped out of the car. They handed me my gun, with the clip removed, and drove away.

I watched them go for a moment, then snapped the clip into my handgun. I started walking, unaware I was still holding the handgun. No one seemed to care. Neither did I.

I approached a Motorcyclist who was standing at the side of the road. I reached his side. Shoved the gun in his face. He got off the bike in a hurry.

"Key?" I demanded.

"It's in the ignition," he pointed to me. "I have two daughters." He pleaded even though I had no intention of harming him.

"Congratulations." I said and roared away on the bike. I saw him in the rearview mirror cover his face with his palms in obvious gratitude to an uncaring God, giving him the credit for him being alive. That credit belonged to me.

I revved the accelerator making the bike lift its front wheels off the ground. I needed to get back to HQ. I needed to talk to Jacob.

Back at HQ, I raced into my office. I had informed the receptionist to locate and send Jacob to me. I was unable to reach him on his mobile.

In my office, I took my handgun, removed the ammo clip and started to pop the bullets out one by one. I took the last one out and unscrewed its bottom. Attached to the bottom, on the inside, was a blinking LED with a receiver and recorder. I removed a thin memory card, and connected it to my computer via an adapter.

I opened a special application which decrypted the contents of the card. Soon, I saw an audio waveform on the screen. I started playing it. It was a recording of the conversation I had just had between Sheru, Sita and myself.

I fast forwarded to the point where I had left the room. And started listening to the recorded conversation.

Sita: Do you think he believed me?

Sheru: It's hard to tell with Abhay. You made your case.

Sita: If we don't stop this plot, the consequences can be severe. It'd throw the entire subcontinent into turmoil.

Sheru: Yes.

Sita: We need to find Priyanka.

Sheru: I know where she is.

Sita: What? Why didn't you tell him?

Sheru: He'd rush in. We need a more strategic extraction.

The blood was rushing to my head. My anger exploded.

"DAMN YOU!" I cursed and slammed my fists onto the table.

Sita: Where is she?

Sheru: She's being held at Hotel Asiana. She's in a penthouse suite. We are monitoring her. We can extract her when it makes most sense.

Sita: You are right, it'd distract and alert everyone. Her life isn't important relative to what we are talking about here anyway.

Sheru: Yes, we need to find out more before we storm the hornet's nest.

I was up, pacing, shoving the bullets back into the magazine. Jacob entered just as the recording ran out.

"That was Sheru's voice. Did you find him?" Jacob asked breathlessly.

"Yes. But he's not relevant. I need to rescue Priyanka."

"You found Priyanka?"

"She's being held at the Asiana. I'm going to go get her. Then you and I, we need to talk."

"Abhay, wait, you need backup."

"No, no backup. I have to do this alone."

"Abhay, we have to plan this!"

I left, leaving Jacob behind, unhappy about this turn of events.

I had a plan. Get Priyanka out of the clutches of these traitors, and then, kill each and every one of them. Sita's sense of justice allowed losing one for many, I'd kill many for the one.

I was always an American in that way.

TWENTY
SECRET REGRETS

I HAD CHEATED ON PRIYANKA. It had happened early on in our marriage. A distant city, a lonely night, a willing woman—we kissed after sharing a beer. It never went beyond that, but the guilt was enough. I had confessed, and although she laughed it off, the incident wedged a distance between us. She once told me, "You're just like everyone else." That stung—I was no different than any other man in her life, all of whom she held in low regard.

If I could take that kiss back, I would. We don't get do-overs in life; actions are irreversible. Our marriage, once dented, became damaged. Bitter exchanges, hurtful taunts, raised hands, slammed doors. We destroyed every happy memory with venom during our fights.

We'd never considered having kids, given the nature of my work with RAW. The plan was to wait until I'd had enough of the field. But now, I wondered if children could have mended or further torn our relationship.

Caught in these thoughts at a red light, the honking horns around me jolted me back to reality. I pushed the Maruti into gear and sped towards the Asiana Hotel, making my way through the two wheelers that had overtaken me. Asiana hotel was around ten kilometers away and it took me around twenty minutes to get there. I pulled into the hotel and had to immediately stop for security. I jumped out of the car.

"I'm in a hurry. My wife is delivering a baby. Park this for me." I left the keys with the guards before they could protest and raced towards the entrance.

I headed to the reception, then changed my mind. I had to assume that the reception was being well paid to alert the occupants of the Penthouse if anyone came looking for them. I decided to take my chances and see if I could figure it out on my own.

I pushed the button for the tenth floor. The doors closed and the elevator started its ride up. Another couple had gotten in with me and had pressed the button for the fourteenth floor. The penthouses were on the fifteenth floor.

The doors opened on the tenth floor, and I took a step out, keeping my hand on the doors. I looked around, didn't see what I was looking for. Got back in the elevator and pressed the button for the eleventh floor. I repeated the same action on that floor annoying my fellow riders.

Same on the twelfth.

"Forgot your floor or what?" the young man remarked in a sarcasm-tinged tone while the woman with him glared at me.

I smiled at them and nodded yes. No point raising a ruckus now. I saw what I wanted on the fourteenth floor. I let the couple get off. They went in the same direction I needed to go. Damn it. They stopped right next to the room that had the room service cart. Damn it again. I walked past them with a smile. They shook their heads rudely and went into their room. I walked back quickly and looked into the room where the room service person was cleaning out the room. He saw me enter and assumed this was my room.

"Just cleaning your room, sir."

I smiled and approached him. A quick move and he lay unconscious on the floor. I searched him quickly for his all-access key. Tied his hands and legs with a couple of bedsheets and improvised a gag. I didn't know how long I needed and I wanted him out of commission for as long as possible.

I stepped out of the room just as the couple exited their room again. I closed the door to the room I was in and allowed them to pass. I walked to the elevator bank behind them. Pressed the up button after they had pressed the down button. They looked at me suspiciously. But I had no choice. I didn't want to waste any more time. Their elevator came first. I had the sinking feeling they were going to flag me as suspicious to the receptionist downstairs. That damn 'if you see something, say something' saying had made its way into India. And people here loved to 'say something' even when there was nothing to say. I mean, I was just a husband trying to rescue his wife. Why can't they leave me alone?

My elevator arrived and I got off at the penthouse level. I scoped the corridors. If I were holding a hostage which penthouse would I pick?

There were eleven penthouses on the floor. I'd ignore every one near the elevator bank. Too much traffic. I'd pick the ones that were corner penthouses and next to a staircase. Only two fit that bill, on opposite sides of the floor.

I walked towards the one on the left, pretending to be a little drunk just incase anyone was watching. Reaching the penthouse, I pretended to have difficulty inserting the card, but I was really listening for any sounds coming from the penthouse, anything that'd rule it in or out. Then I heard it. Children laughing.

This couldn't be it. I pretended to enter the key, realize my mistake when it didn't work, and walked the other way. Towards the other penthouse.

As I passed the elevator bank again, the door to one of the penthouses next to the elevator opened and a white man stepped out. I turned around to evaluate. The man walked to the elevator and pressed the down button. I slowed down wanting him gone before I reached the penthouse where Priyanka likely was. I pretended to stop and dial a number on my cellphone.

I felt it before I saw it, but the movement of the man towards me was lightning fast. He attacked, his jump and kick aimed to knock my head off. I whirled and threw my cellphone in his face, which knocked his rhythm off. I blocked the imprecise punches he threw my way, and kicked him in the stomach.

Two more men, one African-American, and the other Indian, ran out of the penthouse this man had come out of. The Penthouse door on this side of the elevator bank and closest to it also opened and a blonde woman who looked like she was their boss came out from that one. Damn it! They had kept the penthouses closest to the elevators and were surely monitoring every single person who walked past their doors. Too late for that analysis, I attempted to take on this crowd headed my way.

I pulled out my gun which was promptly kicked away. I figured they could kill me and wondered why they didn't.

The fight was getting more intense. I parried the punches from two of the men, then, kicked one in the groin. He went down. But only for a moment. The other I got a knock on the neck and he lay on the floor, incapacitated. The woman, was holding a handgun aimed at me. But she didn't pull the trigger. The indian man yelled at them all.

"Let's go! Let's go! Security is coming up!"

All of them gave me a dirty stare and ran to the other side and took the staircase.

I picked up my handgun. What the hell was going on? Who were they? CIA? MI6? MOSSAD?

I turned around to see Priyanka, being taken by two white men out the door and down the other staircase.

"Priyanka!" I shouted and ran towards them, handgun aimed at them. I couldn't pull the trigger for fear of hitting Priyanka. I reached the door-way, but it was locked. These people were prepared, because there was no lock on the door, they had created something that allowed them to lock it for just such an eventuality.

I pulled on the door, figuring out exactly where the lock was. I stepped back and aimed when, from behind me I heard, "There he is, that's him!"

I turned around to see the young couple with two security guards. They saw my handgun and the woman screamed, "he's got a gun!" And all four of them ran backwards.

I turned back to the door and shot several times and finally got the door open. But those crucial moments were all that these people needed. I ran into the staircase and looked down. Nothing. Then I heard the helicopter.

I wondered if they had run up the stairs. Having seen the capabilities they had shown, I figured that was where they were headed. I rushed up. Again, the door to the rooftop was locked. Damn it. More shots, and I kicked the door open. Only to see the helicopter flying away from the building, and the ladder being pulled back in.

I could see Priyanka through the open door. Our eyes met. "Priyanka!" I shouted. I stood and watched as the helicopter quickly receded into a black dot in the Mumbai sky.

An impotent husband on a rooftop carrying the burden of several secret regrets his wife would never hear from him.

I was sure this would be my last memory of Priyanka. I had blown it. I had lost her forever. The penthouse rooftop became the backdrop for my deepest regret, a silent testimony to a love lost and a husband's failure.

TWENTY-ONE

STILL SKIES

THERE WAS no record of the helicopter. No flight plan had been filed, an enigma in itself.

Equally mystifying was why they hadn't simply killed me. It would have escalated the issue, yes, and perhaps exposed their local operations. But then why not abduct me as well? Was I free because I served a purpose—bait, a distraction, or something else entirely?

Over chai, Jacob and I mulled this over. I speculated aloud, "Maybe they need me out here, perhaps as bait, or as a distraction, or part of their plan."

"The world doesn't revolve around you, Abhay," Jacob remarked, sipping his tea. "Maybe they just wanted to avoid killing. Simple as that."

"But that chopper must've been close by. It got there within minutes," I insisted.

Jacob didn't reply. "You should have waited, Abhay," he said later. "Now, can you please work with me? The PMO is pressing for updates on the assassination plot, and I can't have you running off."

He was right; I'd been a lone ranger, with little to show for it. I had to admit my failure might have cost Priyanka her life, or at least her freedom. I nodded in agreement.

"You're right. We need to track that helicopter. It's our only lead," I conceded.

Jacob sighed. "You think I haven't already started looking into it? The word has gone out already. I'm doing my job. When will you start doing yours? The life of our PM is in our hands and you are off doing your own thing. I need a team player, Abhay. Are you going to be one or not?"

I put my hand on his shoulder in an attempt to calm him down, but Jacob just shook my hand off. This was the first time I had seen Jacob annoyed at me. I had believed rescuing Priyanka was the key to solving all of this. I had failed in doing so.

"I'm on the team." I reassured Jacob. "Let's do this."

"We need to understand the PM's itinerary, identify weak spots, come up with a defense plan. If everything Sheru told you is true, then, the attack will happen prior to the election."

I nodded. This was the kind of work we normally did at RAW. Research and Analysis. The kind of active field work I had engaged in was an exception.

"I've setup a meeting with the PM Security Force today. Let's get all the details from them, make our recommendations, and plan out a strategy." Jacob seemed engaged now, and more relaxed now that he had a sense of control.

It was not fun trying to understand the PM's schedule. Election year in the most normal times was still the most chaotic for any political party in India, not to speak of the electorate, but the ruling party, specially if it was struggling to hold onto its power had a tough time. They had to mitigate their failures, attack the opposing parties, and still paint a rosy figure.

This was a worse situation. The Lok Sabha, which is the house of representatives chosen by direct election was headed towards dissolution because a splinter group that had provided the necessary support to the ruling party to be able to form the government was withdrawing its support. Elections for all seats of the Lok Sabha were scheduled for December 11th, less than two months away.

The fact was that there was no real schedule we could plan around. The PM was doing what was needed to make the case to the people to reelect his party in a strength that'd allow him to form a government without requiring the support of another political party. The chances were slim to none. But that assumed that the elections would be fair and without fraud. A very big, and in many ways, naive assumption.

I was searching for a pattern in the PMs schedule that confirmed the theory Sita and Sheru had proposed. I figured if there were something like that in the works, there'd be meetings setup. Something like this could not happen without conversations. It was hard to say, but there seemed to be a few blackout dates and times in the PMs schedule that seemed to be possible candidates for such meetings.

Then again, they could simply be some personal engagements.

One appointment stood out. The PM was not attending a major meet of the party leaders a week from today. Instead, he was going to be in Mumbai at the time. That felt odd simply because the agenda for the Mumbai trip was unclear. In addition, there was no close family of the PM in Mumbai.

I made a mental note and marked off that slot as a possible item to discuss with Jacob.

The other worrisome item was the number of chopper trips the PM took to various locations to deliver speeches supporting his party's campaign. After my last chopper encounter, it was clear that the enemy had substantial air support. If they decided to take out the PMs helicopter in the air, there'd be precious little we could do to prevent it. After all, India's Prime Minister did not fly around in the relative safety afforded to the US President on Air Force One.

I felt I had enough to go on for now. Jacob could chew over this information and determine if there was a plan of action that made sense. I figured we'd end up having to involve a number of other security groups and had no desire to be the one to coordinate them all. I'd leave that to Jacob to assign to some task force. Frankly, if the PM indeed was planning to sell off India's premier intelligence organization to a foreign power, any foreign power, then I really did not care what happened to him.

I got in my car and took off for Jacob's residence.

As I had promised myself, I had put the word out regarding the helicopter and the information I was seeking. I got a lead from the most unexpected place. A farmer from a coastal village had complained to the local Panchayat, the village governance unit, that a helicopter had ruined his peaceful night when it landed near his house and had essentially damaged the straw roof on his house. But that wasn't all. A black Land Rover - based on his description and his insistence it wasn't a Tata Sumo - had arrived to pick up the passengers, and then, the helicopter had flown off God knows where.

With the coordinates of that man's village in my hands, I was pretty sure I'd get a fix on a radar map somewhere that'd tell me where that Helicopter had gone to. I had already gotten the word out to ensure we were getting all the info we could on the Land Rover.

It was the helicopter lead that panned out first. A dear friend in the Aviation Research Center had correlated several radar archives to determine that there was indeed a flight that went from the location the farmer had indicated to an Agricultural University, "India-US Agricultural Research University," that was financed by a grant from a United States benefactor, and indeed this University did have two helicopters on staff, ostensibly to cover the large land area they covered.

What brought it all together was a call from the PMO. I had asked them a question about the PMs trip to Mumbai. They confirmed that he was indeed coming to Mumbai to inaugurate a new wing of the residential complex at the "India-US Agricultural Research University."

This whole setup smelled of the CIA.

I pulled to the side of the road to digest this news. This was big. This was possibly beyond me. I tried calling Jacob again, but he didn't answer the phone. I put the Maruti into gear and swerved back into traffic. I needed to talk to Jacob asap and figured the best way was to go to his home, and meet him there, or wait there until he returned from where ever he had gone.

Jacob lived in a residential part of Mumbai. Although his job exposed Jacob to a lot of money, and I mean a lot, in his life outside, Jacob lived a life of modest means. He was an ethical man. He tried his best to live his life according to the principles his mother had instilled in him from the time that he was a little boy without a father, trying to make his way in the world.

I was lucky to have a handler like him.

I reached Brindavan Apartments named after the famed gardens where Krishna, the warrior God of the Mahabharata lived. Although Jacob was Christian, he had read the Bhagavad Gita, the discourse that Krishna gives to Arjuna, which lays out, in simplistic terms, the nature of life and the purpose of existence. Jacob frequently quoted the Gita and had several phrases from it, all written in the now rarely used Sanskrit language.

I parked in a guest spot and took the stairs to the first floor. On the landing, I took a left and headed all the way down to Jacob's apartment. On the doorknob, there was a blue bag. Left there for the milk delivery person to leave the milk packets in there. I looked inside and there were two of them. It seemed like Jacob was either not at home or was fast asleep.

I knocked a few times, rang the bell and then, waited. I tried calling him again.

No response.

This was odd. I could never remember a time when Jacob had not answered my call. I went downstairs to check with the security guard if he had seen Jacob. He said no, but told me Jacob's car was in the garage. I went to check the car. Indeed, it was still there. I wondered if Jacob had just gotten tired and was in deep sleep. I quickly dismissed that option. Jacob was a light sleeper and this had never happened before.

I dialed his number again.

I heard a phone ring.

From the trunk of Jacob's car.

My adrenaline started racing. Why would Jacob leave his phone in the trunk of his car?

That phone was like an additional body part to Jacob. Where his phone was, there Jacob would be.

I stared at the trunk, paralyzed by the thought that had just formed in my head. I knew I had to open the trunk.

I yelled out to the security guard and asked him to get a crowbar. He appeared in less than twenty seconds with one. I put it under the lid of the trunk and applied pressure. The door popped open.

The smell hit me first.

Then, Jacob's eyes -- lifeless, starting dead ahead. They seemed to be looking at me as if to say I had come there too late.

Between his accusing eyes was a bullet entry wound. His body had been unceremoniously dumped in the trunk, his neck contorted. No living person, no great Yogi, could have remained still in that position for even a short period of time.

Jacob had been dead for several hours. But his body would no longer give him any discomfort.

Everything had gone silent as all the background noise faded away for me. A lone bird and its mating call broke through my deadened senses. Then, I heard the voice. I could never forget it.

"Abhay." It was Goru. I whirled around and looked, but I didn't see anyone. Confused, I started looking above me, under the car, but no one.

"Abhay, listen carefully." There it was again. It was like hearing voices in my head.

"There's a communication device we've planted behind your ear." The voice was in my head! I felt behind both ears. Behind my right, I felt just the tiny feel of a scar. Damn it! This is what was put in when I was captured and clearly operated upon.

But Jacob had done a full scan. He'd never have missed it. Unless, he was with them all along. I looked at Jacob's dead eyes, trying to pry his secrets out of him. Nothing made sense.

"What do you want?" I responded.

"Good, I can hear you. Everything is still working correctly. We'll be in constant touch now. We've been hearing everything you've been hearing so far, obviously. "

"If you have hurt Priyanka..." I began, gritting my teeth. Goru interrupted me, "she's alive. For now. Whether she continues to live, depends on whether you cooperate or not."

"What do you want?" It was time to start playing this game these people had thought they had under control.

"We want to meet you. It'd be best if you come to us."

"Why me?"

"Because you are the only one within RAW we can trust."

I didn't understand. I went through Jacob's jacket pockets and took out his cell phone.

"Did you kill Jacob?" I asked as I went through the recent calls on Jacob's cell. There was one number that showed up as "Laundry" which I didn't recognize.

"No," Goru responded. "But we want to know who did."

I hit SEND. And I heard the ringing on the other end. This was Goru's number.

"Jacob was working with you," I said.

"No. But we had tried to warn him. Come to the east end of the Andheri Fly Bridge. We'll talk more in person."

I was going to play along.

For now.

TWENTY-TWO
SHATTERED BONES, SHUTTERED SOUL

BEFORE LEAVING, I resolved to remove their implanted device. I found a standard-issue knife in Jacob's shoe and, despite the blood and pain, I managed to extract a small plastic device from behind my ear, designed to pass unnoticed by scans.

It wasn't Jacob's oversight. I opened the car's back door, carefully moved Jacob's body from the trunk to the backseat, stiff with rigor mortis.

I drove to our discreet facility—by day a funeral home, by night our place for disposing of the aftermath of missions. This was my first time delivering a colleague.

Upon arrival, Vivek, the director, had his team swiftly move Jacob's body away. After explaining the circumstances, he assured me he'd handle the formalities and inform Jacob's family.

Puzzled over Jacob's murder, I reviewed our recent interactions for clues, finding none. I reached the bridge, a snarl of traffic echoing my internal chaos. This meeting point left me exposed, vulnerable to being watched or worse—another assassination attempt. Yet I had to risk it; avenues were closing, and I needed a breakthrough.

I called Goru.

"Why is the device off?" he inquired.

I couldn't help but smirk. "Destroyed it. Call this number if you want to talk. I like my privacy."

Goru's frustration was palpable. "That device was crucial for future coordination."

I bristled. "You don't get to decide what goes in my body." Taking a breath, I cut the childish back-and-forth. "I'm here. Where are you?"

"Behind you," he said.

I spun to find Goru by a sedan, gesturing me over. "Let's talk inside."

I had one burning question: "Where's Priyanka?"

"In the car," he said, a statement I met with skepticism until I saw her— really saw her—inside the car, offering a rueful smile.

"Priyanka, are you okay?" I asked as she nodded, tears brimming.

She nodded. Tears started to well up in her eyes.

That was when the first bullet hit me in the arm. There was no sound, which meant the shots were coming from a distant sniper rifle or were silenced or both. I fell to the ground, both from the hit and to protect myself and gain some protection from the body of the car.

The next shot hit Goru, right between the eyes. He was dead before he hit the ground next to me.

Priyanka shouted -- "Get in!"

She rushed to the door and tried to pull me in.

"Hell no!" I shouted back. I had seen a glint off what must have been a sniper's sight on the bridge. Then a moving form. The sniper. Damned if I was going to let this guy go.

The driver had come out and was dragging Goru's body into the sedan, trying to stay low and out of the line of fire.

I headed out towards the bridge keeping out of the line of fire and hoping there wasn't a secondary sniper who could get me from a different angle. Seems I had lucked out on that front.

Priyanka shouted after me, I couldn't make out what she was saying, but it didn't matter. It was clear where I was headed. She'd figure it out. I took a look back at the car. The driver had pulled Goru in and shut the door. Several bullets hit the car which, I realized was, bulletproof.

They were safe there for the moment. I ran towards the bridge. I saw the sniper starting to descend from his nest. He was dressed in a grey metal suit, which hid him well against the metallic color of the bridge. He was fast, this guy.

I picked up my pace, now that I knew he wasn't aiming at me. I got to the edge of the bridge and jumped on the outside edge, which was about ten inches wide. All I needed to run towards the sniper and keep out of sight. I wondered if he had seen me.

I wanted to throw him off his rhythm. I shouted, "Hey! You!" He heard me. He turned. Watched me approaching. My Glock handgun aimed at him. He waited for me. I saw that he was wearing a scarf and headwear. Only his eyes would have shown, but with the dark sunglasses he was wearing, there was nothing to make out.

"I will shoot if you move a muscle." I yelled out. He was still. Too still for my taste. I approached closer. He began to raise his hand. I saw then that he was holding a grenade. I was close enough to see that the pin was removed. If he let go of the liver, I guessed we had about five seconds before it exploded. I was close enough to be killed by it.

"Don't do it! You don't have to die." I felt silly saying that. But I stopped. I didn't want to be blown up. I could shoot him, but then I wouldn't have my live suspect to interrogate for information. I was pretty sure this guy was willing to blow himself up.

Suddenly, his arm swung away and the grenade fell. He was shot. I turned to see Priyanka, holding a Glock standing on the bridge side. I moved quickly towards the sniper and grabbed him just as he was trying to raise his rifle with his good hand. One punch to the face, then, another to rip away his headgear.

The grenade exploded on the dry river bed below, which at the spot we were at, was comprised entirely of stone.

He turned and punched me before I could get a good look at him. He kicked me in the leg and I almost lost my balance. I was about to fall onto the rocks below, when he grabbed me. And pushed me back to safety. Our eyes met then.

"Sheru." I said the word softly. The surprise was complete. "Why?"

"You'll never understand," he said. Then, he jumped. A base jump parachute opened up. It was too short a height, but clearly Sheru was prepared. He landed with enough slowing of his velocity to be able to walk away.

Priyanka was next to me within moments. She aimed her handgun.

"Don't shoot. It's Sheru," I said.

Her face registered shock. Then, she put her handgun back in her holster and pulled me up.

"Who do you work for?" I asked.

"Later," she said and forced me to run towards the sedan which had come onto the bridge now. We got into the backseat.

I saw Goru propped up in the front seat.

"He's dead." The driver informed us of this useless fact.

Priyanka turned to me. "How did they know?"

"How did who know?" I asked.

"Unit 13. CIA." she replied, anger welling up in her.

I looked at her. She was so different from the demure Priyanka I knew. She looked tougher somehow. She looked in command. She looked like a woman capable of carrying and using a firearm. The Glock in a front holster. My wife, carrying a firearm.

"Who are you?" I asked.

"Later, Abhay." She replied tersely.

"NOW!" I shouted. "Who do you work for?"

"CIA." She replied in a tired voice, and shattered my small, dreamy and perfect little domestic life for all of eternity.

TWENTY-THREE
THE HUMMINGBIRD SPEAKS

"W**HY DID** the chicken cross the road?" asked the portly man, his lips curving into a smile as he arranged Goru's body on the cold, metallic tray, readying for autopsy.

"Because of bad intel," he answered his own riddle, laughter bellowing from his belly.

I stood there next to Priyanka and two men likely tasked with shooting me if I acted up.

"So what were we?" I asked.

"We were just... part of my job." She said, with no trace of contrition in her voice.

"Spoken like a true American." I sent it back to her with a dash of bile.

"Look, it wasn't like you had any feeling left for me, so let's not pretend we are walking around with broken hearts here. And in case, my colleague is dead. You are not. It's not the same thing."

"I could have been," I offered. "A little to the left, and he'd have shot me in the heart."

"Didn't know you had one."

Ouch. Separation did not make our hearts grow fonder.

"Will someone tell me what's going on?" I switched topics to something less contentious.

"If you start acting like a professional, maybe." She was on a roll.

"Since you haven't killed me yet, I suppose I am able to try. You wanted me for something, so perhaps we can get on with it."

"Fine." She replied curtly.

"Just one question, Priyanka. And I think I deserve a truthful answer. Just this one question."

"No, I never loved you."

"That's not the question."

"Oh"

Hell hath no fury like a man ridiculed by his bad-ass wife who regards him with a lop-sided grin, amused by his pathetic need for a hug.

I pushed down my fury. Let it go to hell. I asked my question.

"Your fascination with hummingbirds, was that for real, or was that part of your act?"

"That's your question? Does it matter?" she asked.

"Yeah. It matters. I hated those things all over the apartment."

She smiled. "I love hummingbirds. I really do."

"Ok, in that case, I'll leave them where they are."

I smiled back. She bit her lip. We dropped the small talk. We were professionals now. Not husband and wife.

"I'll fill you in." She said, as she turned and led me away.

"Only took you five years to get around to it." I couldn't resist that jibe.

She was able to resist responding. Dammit. She was always the stronger one in our relationship.

———

"I'VE BEEN UNDERCOVER for too long. I never expected it to go anywhere. I was never asked for any information. The Indian services were easy enough to penetrate to use me for that. I suppose I was a trump card, to be used when the stakes got really high. And this time, they did."

Priyanka downed an Espresso as she laid it out for me. Just the two of us. No guards. But I suppose there were listening devices galore keeping us company.

"There's a splinter CIA group that was trying to do something which could trigger war. They were trying to usurp an entire intelligence organization after having bought over the ruling Prime Minister of the country. Their goal was simple. To use the organization to do things they couldn't. Assassinations. Spying on China. Iran. Saudi Arabia. Places they had trouble getting into. This would be their proxy unit."

"How much money are we talking about?"

"They had money. It was a reserve set aside after 9/11. They had enough. But they didn't just use money. Blackmail was an added leverage. But it's one thing to buy an organization out, and another to convince everyone working there to do one thing versus another."

"How did they hope to achieve that?"

"By bringing in nine men they had identified and controlled from the Indian Police Services, the Indian Army, who were frustrated with the government's blocking of their intelligence efforts against China and Pakistan. The government wanted good relations, and they were foregoing strategic advantage for short term PR gain."

"And the PM's assassination plot?"

"It'd be the final icing on the cake. It would be the act that'd terrorize the nation, and allow for greater, unfettered operational advantages for this agency, now under their control."

"Sounds really ambitious."

"Yes, and we got wind of it when one of their agents, killed one of ours. Brother killing brother. We tracked him into our organization, and then the trial disappeared. All we were able to get was that there was a Unit 13 out there, and it appeared to have gone rogue with a lot of money."

"So Sheru is one of them?"

"We are not certain. There seems to be a RAW group we were unaware of. They are being targeted by Unit 13 and are being eliminated. Your name was on there."

"I was not part of any secret group with RAW." I wondered if she was referring to the CHAKS unit, but then, some of the others killed didn't seem to be part of it.

"Then you were a candidate for joining it." Priyanka spoke softly, and her voice was commanding, calm. So different from the arguments we had had, screaming matches in fact, as husband and wife.

She continued. "We wanted to track you, see who met you. We thought that this group would try to recruit you given how high the stakes have gotten, but no one seems to have."

That was when I thought about Sita. She had not tried to recruit me in the least. But she was the only new element in the mix. But she seemed to be with Sheru. And clearly, an agent for the GIP.

I tried to wrap my head around it all. The thing with trying to figure this out, was that you needed a frame of reference. You needed a frame of reference not just for who your friends were and who your enemies were, but you needed one just for good and evil, right and wrong. Everyone here seemed to be struggling to do something to fight who or what they thought was evil, but the other party felt the same way about them. In times like these, I suppose it comes down to your own value system.

I had to make a choice. Do I protect the elected leader of this country, who was trying to sell out the entire intelligence agency to a foreign power even as he was being shown the door, or do I focus only on stopping this plot?

In my view, I had to do both.

"How far will your organization go to stop your splinter unit?" I asked Priyanka.

"Far. Very far. But the thing is, we don't know if we'll be successful in ever rooting it out. We may chop off a few heads, but that'll be it."

"What do you know about the PMs visit to the university?"

She thought for a moment, wondering how much she should tell me here. "Well, the university is a front for Unit 13. That much we know. But not all the employees are in on the real goal. It does function as a real university. There are, we think, three people who represent the interests of Unit 13. Their meetings will not be on the agenda, or if they are, will be disguised well. If the PM makes it there, we believe he'll sign and approve the transfers of several personnel which will be the first step of the transition."

"And in return the PMs Swiss bank account is fattened up." I groaned.

"Substantially," Priyanka confirmed.

"Switzerland is the real enemy." I said flippantly.

"We use them. They are a tool, and like any tool, it can be used or misused." Priyanka replied calmly.

Priyanka had a way of making me feel like I was a petulant child. And I had a way of not being able to shake it off.

"Sure. Let's you and me open a joint account then."

She shook her head and rolled her eyes. Typical Priyanka.

"What we don't know," she continued, "is where and when the assassination will take place. The assumption should be it'll be before the PM can make these transfers formal. This is what we assume the secret RAW team is trying to prevent."

I started going over the PM schedule I was going to discuss with Jacob. And it hit me. The perfect location for the assassination attempt could be his upcoming visit to the Delhi Zoo, just before his trip to Mumbai.

TWENTY-FOUR
JOCULAR ELEPHANTS

The one-seventy-six acre Delhi Zoo was a favorite for Delhi's families, especially the kids.

The Prime Minister's visit was set for a Children's Day event, a brief appearance really, just a photo op with scripted media soundbites, which the media, much in the ruling party's pocket, would broadcast under the guise of news in exchange for hefty advertising commitments from corporate allies.

The symbiotic extortion system between the media and the political class had become increasingly apparent. Negative news would dominate the airwaves relentlessly until financial deals were struck, after which the news cycle would miraculously pivot to an announcement of a "committee" to investigate, and then silence. An effective, if parasitic, system in a nation where the common man felt both apathetic and powerless, it provided a lucrative modus operandi for the manipulative few.

In essence, the political and media landscapes in India were their own distinct zoos, hosting a curious collection of creatures.

Priyanka had introduced me to John, likely a pseudonym given its commonality. Ostensibly a corporate liaison, John was actually a CIA operative providing logistical support on the ground.

John was privy to the assassination plot. Seemingly amiable, but in our line of work, that meant little. Other peripheral figures dotted the operation's landscape, but Priyanka dealt with them, now fully embodying her American persona.

I recalled Sita's remarks about Priyanka's New York education.

"There's much I don't know about you. Yet, I have no option but trust."

She smirked. "You have every reason to distrust me."

"What will I tell our friends?" I half-joked, trying to lighten the mood.

Her smile waned. "I'm sorry about Tony," she said, and I could only offer a nonchalant shrug.

"The bomb wasn't your doing, I presume?"

"No, we were trying to keep you safe. It likely came from Sheru's end."

"Likely," I agreed.

News of Jacob's death had my office frantically reaching out, but I paid it little mind until a contact from NASR hinted at a manhunt for me.

I wasn't keen on confinement to an interrogation room, debating the urgency of the plot.

I'd rather be rogue and active than a handcuffed yet compliant citizen.

That afternoon's flight to Delhi in a private jet, courtesy of the CIA, carried a silent Priyanka and me. I pondered over her true identity during our marriage. Was any part of our shared life genuine? If she now professed love, could I forgive and set her free? I doubted the largeness of my heart.

Our reconnaissance at the zoo made it clear—if the PM was to be hit there, we could only thwart it by canceling his visit.

Priyanka proposed a bomb threat to cancel the event without raising suspicions. Sensible, yet it would relinquish our certainty of the attackers' timing.

Sharing my reservations, she understood. Passing the Elephant Area, one's trumpet seemed almost like laughter.

"What if we deployed a decoy?" I mused.

"A double for a PR event?" she queried.

"We have a convincing double for such occasions," she revealed, a standard CIA practice.

The incredulity of it all made me question the logistics.

"We don't suggest; we implement," she clarified.

"And the real PM?" I probed.

"We'll ensure he's... delayed."

"Kidnapping?"

"More like delaying against his wishes."

Treason loomed over me.

"Is this our sole option?"

"The best one if we aim to catch the attacker," she insisted.I thought about it.

The plan sucked. It was the stupidest thing to ever contemplate. I had no belief it'd work.

But when you have no options, the world of reason and logic turns inside out. And even Elephants trumpeting sounds like laughter.

So I told Priyanka we'll do it.

Priyanka told me she had already kicked that plan into action. She had only wanted to see if I'd have reached the same conclusion she did. For once, we had agreed upon something, when we had not during our entire marriage. What else could I do but laugh, and join the elephants in their jolly?

While in Delhi, I called up my contact at the PMO, but he refused to talk to me. Apparently, the word was out that I had either defected or been turned, and the standing order was to bring me in. Alive, if possible.

We returned to Mumbai that night.

I watched Priyanka as she stared out the window. Who was she? What had she been during our marriage? Was any of what we had shared real?

I knew the games we played, but what she had done was beyond anything I'd ever be capable of.

Perhaps that was something I liked to believe, and I was, in reality, capable of much worse.

What if she told me now that she had experienced love for me in our marriage? What would I do? Would I forgive her everything? Set her free? Did I really have such a big heart?

I don't think so.

TWENTY-FIVE
ASSETS AND TARGETS

RETURNING TO MUMBAI, Priyanka and I began crafting a strategy. Our objective: discern a method to identify members of RAW's clandestine faction and find a channel to reach them.

John, backed by another team I wasn't privy to, was concurrently compiling a dossier on potential CIA operatives within India who might be targeting RAW agents.

I was intent on reconnecting with Sheru. Signals were sent out; if he wished to meet, he'd find a way.

The depth of CIA's infiltration into RAW astonished me. Access to information now made me feel as if I was an insider with top-level clearance. My familiarity with RAW's current methods enabled me to code and run algorithms that sought out patterns and generated leads.

Two individuals emerged as potential insiders of this covert RAW faction. Their travel habits contradicted their supposed cessation from field duty.

Deciding to confront them directly, we learned one was abroad, the other resided in Goa. We caught a flight to Goa's Dabolim Airport.

We reached Dabolim around two in the afternoon.

Goa's serene landscape, a stark contrast to Mumbai's bustle, had been our honeymoon retreat five years prior. It was the best time I had had in my life. We had stayed in an older house that was built by the Portuguese and had that old style feel, and hospitality we were very appreciative of. If Priyanka was thinking about the same thing, she didn't give any indication of it. She seemed to be fixated on our mission, undistracted by nostalgia.

We had a car waiting and immediately set off to meet our first target. We reached too late. We saw him being carried away in a funeral procession. We learnt from a member of the funeral procession that he had committed suicide two days ago by blowing his brains out with his service revolver.

Neither Priyanka nor I believed that was a suicide. But there was little we could do at this stage. We turned the car around to head back to the airport. We reached the airport and returned the car. We stepped out of the car rental office and noticed an army truck parked in front.

"Hey!" a deep male voice boomed out from behind us.

Priyanka and I both turned. An Army Officer with two soldiers beside him, was waving at the truck. We turned back to see the truck reversing and coming closer to us.

"Keep walking towards the truck." The voice, now conversational, was right behind us. The jab of the muzzle of their automatic weapons denied us an argument.

"Are you sure you have the right people?" I shook my head, suggesting they were making a huge mistake.

"Didn't you just go to meet my friend... who they say shot himself with his service revolver?" The officer's voice was laced with anger and sadness.

"Yes. Are you...", I didn't get a chance to finish my question.

"Get in the truck. It's your choice whether you do it alive or dead." The thread in the officer's voice was irrefutable. Priyanka and I reached the truck and climbed up, assisted by the soldiers inside the truck. The officer and his two soldiers climbed in behind us and the truck roared off.

The officer sat in front of us glaring at us. His soldiers positioned themselves near the back of the truck. No friendly looks from them either. I thought the best of asking questions. Army people admired bravery and action, not talk. I decided to hold onto my questions until we had a better feel for where this was headed.

The truck seemed headed outside the civil enclave that housed the airport. The rest of the area was really owned by the Navy, although the Army had sections of it too. We were in an area that seemed to be a Cantonment. Army presence was everywhere. We were stopped at several check posts, but the very sight of the Officer was sufficient to get us unhindered passage.

This cantonment was not the destination. We simply passed through. I suspect it was to ensure we were not being followed. Soon, we had left the Cantonment behind and were driving on the road leading to Vasco da Gama City just over three kilometers away.

On the outskirts of the city, we made a sharp right off the main road and parked in the area behind a church.

The officer got out first. Two of his soldiers got down and stood guard while we made our way down. I helped Priyanka down and we stood face to face with the officer.

"It'd be best if you turned over all your weapons now. The temptation to use them might get too strong for you. I can assure you the effort will simply get you killed." He said.

I had no desire to argue. I held out my Glock, barrel to the ground, and handed it over to one of the soldiers who stepped forward to take it. Priyanka handed over hers too.

"If you had wanted to just kill us, you missed way too many chances. I am guessing you want to talk. There's very little time. The sooner the better." I said.

The officer nodded. "Come with me."

He gestured to the soldiers to stay behind and the three of us walked up the steps and through the massive doors into the Church.

The Officer walked us over to the area where disciples' lit candles currying favor with God. He lit one. "For my murdered colleague." He said simply. I lit one too. Priyanka followed suit. I guess we all needed favors, me most of all.

We stood in silence for a minute.

The Officer broke the silence first. "Abhay, there's a takedown order out for you."

"I know." I shrugged. "I wasn't going to go in and get trapped in a room answering questions while people were getting killed around me."

"I like your style."

"It's not as good as yours." I reparteed.

He laughed. "Well, I'm sorry to bring you here this way, but there's no other way to make sure that you were not just bait dangled in front of me."

"What's going on?" I asked.

"I was hoping you could tell me." He responded.

I looked at Priyanka. She dove right in. "There's a plot to kill the Prime Minister."

"Combined with a plot by a rogue CIA outfit to essentially take over the reigns of RAW." I interjected.

"I know about both. What else can you tell me?" The officer replied.

"Then maybe you can tell us why these RAW agents are being killed and by whom?" Priyanka asked him.

"We are part of a special group within RAW. Most of RAW is federated or it reports to a clear hierarchy. We are special. We have a clear group that reports to no one except ourselves. We are independent..."

I interrupted him. "You are rogue!"

For a moment, I thought I had offended him. But he just laughed. "Yes, you can call us that. We have no oversight. But in this country, do you really think any of the oversight mechanisms have worked?"

He left that question hanging in the air and I had to nod in understanding. He continued. "We work by consensus. If that makes you feel any better. We test our candidates extensively before we invite them to the group and then put them on probation for a long time before we accept them. So its not a dictatorship. It's democracy, but not representative."

"Why are you being targeted?" Priyanka asked again. She clearly wanted to get to the point.

"We have a mole in the CIA. We have a mole in the group that has hatched the plot to take over the reigns of RAW to be more specific. We don't know their every move now, as they have gone on the defensive, but to progress their plan, they have to let out information, and we will get it. We will have it before they can find the mole and we can sabotage their plan. And once this PM is kicked out in the election, which we expect will happen, their plan will end. And an opportunity may never arise again."

"So they want to kill you, and render the mole useless as they will have no one to pass info to." Priyanka completed that thought.

"Yes. The moment the mole tries to establish any new contact with any other agency or individual, the mole will be exposed. We have the power to block this. The PM will not be able to push any of the people he's selected into the organization, not if we have anything to do with it."

"How many people are left in your group?"

"Besides me?" The officer bent his head as if the burden of the world had finally caught up to him. "Besides me... just one. We are willing to give our life for our country..."

We were interrupted by a sharp burst of automatic fire. Then, shouts from the soldiers. Then, silence.

"They are under attack!" The officer took out his handgun. "The attackers must have silenced weapons."

That would explain the lack of shots. Shit. And we had no weapons.

"Drop the gun, Major." Priyanka's voice was level and even. I turned to her. She had a small gun that she must have hid somewhere on her body. "Drop it."

The Major face twisted in rage. He raised his gun but before he could fire, several shots from a silenced automatic pistol took him out.

His dead body fell at my feet. I turned to see who the attackers were.

Sheru!

Following close behind him was John.

Working together? I didn't understand. My brain tried to think furiously fast, but it didn't get anywhere. I turned just in time to see Priyanka's hand come down to strike me on my head.

I tried to avoid her blow.

I failed.

Once again, everything went black. This was becoming a bad habit.

TWENTY-SIX
WHEN DOGS CRY

I DON'T KNOW how long I remained unconscious. When I came to, I could hear Priyanka's voice, shouting at someone outside. I grabbed the dead officer's gun and rushed out.

I saw Priyanka heading away after examining one of the dead soldiers.

"Stop!" I yelled out. She didn't stop. She kept running. I had no choice. I raised my gun. I took aim. My finger wrapped around the trigger. But I never pulled it. I watched her instead. Running away from me. She turned back one final time as she slowed down to a stop.

We looked at each other across the distance. It wasn't that much if you measured it with a tape. But then that sedan pulled around the corner, door open. She got into it. A man reached out to close the door. It was Sheru. Unmistakably Sheru, wearing dark sunglasses and a suit.

In that moment, I knew we were light years apart.

The sedan pulled away. Now, my anger surged and I pulled that trigger. The bullets flew out of my handgun, all fourteen of them. All impotent against the bulletproof sedan. I watched mutely as it drove past me. She and Sheru, together, hidden behind the darkened windows.

I emptied the magazine then threw the gun behind the disappearing sedan as it drove away in the dying night. I ran after it. I don't know how long I ran.

Day turned into night. It was the barking dogs that finally brought me back to reality.

I found myself surrounded by a pack of stray dogs. I was all alone on this street. I had invaded their territory.

One of them started to get aggressive and moved closer, sharp barks and canines bared.

I hissed at it. In that moment, I was an animal. I was one of them. I got them. I understood their way. I was not supposed to make eye contact, but right now, I wanted to let this dog know that tonight, I didn't care. Tonight, I was a destroyed soul and it could do me no harm. There was nothing left to harm.

I took two steps forward. Hissing and making guttural sounds. I knew that if I laid hands on that mutt, I'd kill it. I didn't want to. It snapped at me a few times, running around in circles, undecided if I was a threat or a joke. Then, taking no chances, it moved away. The others followed its lead and I was left alone.

Alone with my tears.

Several headlights on the road. I got off the road and hid. Army trucks all heading towards the Church. I knew the entire area would be swarming with Army personnel all riled up, angry, and committed to track down the killers. I figured if I managed to make it to Vasco da Gama City, I'd have a place to hide, to think and find a way out of this.

I continued to walk towards the city. I continued to think about what had just happened.

Sheru and Priyanka were working together. What did that mean? They were both CIA. Worse, they were the rogue CIA outfit. Which meant that the Agriculture University probably had a few of their men on its payroll, but was not an all-out CIA funded organization. Which meant that the CIA had no clue about any of this!

I passed a house and I could make out the breaking news on the TV. It caught my eye, as my picture was on the screen. I walked closer and saw my mug with the word, "Suspect", under it. Great. So they had planted the idea that I had killed the Officer. Perhaps that's what Priyanka was doing when she was examining the soldier. Perhaps she was placing my gun there.

If the plan was to make me look like the one responsible for the PM's assassination, then, the current RAW leadership would be deprived of all power to question the PM's appointments.

All the appointments the PM had made would sail through. Not one representative would have the guts to counter them. Sheru and Priyanka were in this together. I was played. From the very beginning. This plan was five years in the making.

I was so fucked. But if I didn't do anything to stop this, India was going to be really fucked up. More so than it ever had been.

I wasn't about to let that happen.

TWENTY-SEVEN
EYE OF THE TIGER

Vasco da Gama did what Christopher Columbus set out to do. Find a sea route from Europe to India. This route was well-known to the traders who travelled between Africa and India, and it was one of them who piloted Gama to India. What Gama brought then was the beginning of the colonization of India. In many ways, colonization may have gone away as a governing structure, but it still existed in so many other ways.

The city that was a namesake for Vasco da Gama was small and not very impressive. I walked over towards the railway station.

My initial thought had been to go to the railway station and take a train back to Mumbai. The contingent of Army soldiers in front of the station put an end to that line of thinking.

I considered reaching out to one of my old associates. The problem was I was completely unsure if he'd help me or turn me in. I figured I'd take a chance. After all, I was an easy target at this point and could expect no help from any of my traditional contacts.

But the funny thing about contacts was that you could always make new ones. Goa was a major port with access to the ocean which made it a haven for criminals and smugglers. One of the better known was Basu, a Bengali intellectual-turned-criminal. He was known for his exhaustive knowledge of history, which in fact, he turned to his use and used as justification for all his criminal acts. RAW had had him on the radar for a while, but had not moved in, because he seemed to have contacts with criminals and terrorist cells based out of the Middle East. Mossad was very interested in him but had held off on RAW's insistence that Basu was more useful free than captive, alive than dead. Basu continued on his merry way, blissfully ignorant of the thin threads of need that kept him out of harm's way.

Today, I was ready to cut those threads to get what I wanted.

Weary of walking, I appropriated a bicycle—no gem, but a means to an end. The owner, unconcerned with security for such a decrepit item, hadn't bothered with a lock. To me, however, it was a treasure that facilitated my escape, navigating turns to elude potential pursuit.

I cycled away on this Atlas cycle, remembering the days as a young boy, and my first attempts at riding this bike sitting on the seat, when my feet weren't even long enough to touch the ground.

Basu would give me weapons, men, money and better transport. I'd give him this bike and his life in return. Fair trade.

A seven-kilometer ride later, I reached a seaside villa. Basu's residence. He made no attempt at living a secret life. Why should he? He had paid off just about everybody who needed to be paid off.

I took the bike right up to the gate. His guards looked at me like I had landed from Mars. No one had ridden up to that gate in anything less than a Mercedez Benz in the time they had worked there. And here I was, Atlas bicycle by my side, walking up to them. Only my demeanor and clothes stopped them from shooing me away.

They looked at each other, unsure of how to treat me.

"Tell Basu Bhai I want to meet him." I said in as commanding a voice as one can muster up when they are standing next to an Atlas bicycle.

The Chief Security guard looked me over, and at the bicycle, making it clear to me that he thought I wasn't worthy.

"Who are you?"

"Sir!" I said.

"What?" He asked.

"Who are you, SIR?" I emphasized. "Next time you ask me a question without 'sir' at the end, I'll make sure Basu bhai feeds you to Surpanakha."

Surpanakha was the catalyst character in the epic Ramayana that set the story in motion by instigating her brother to kidnap Sita. Basu had a pet crocodile bearing her name, and the legend was that he'd feed his crocodile his enemies and friends who crossed him, after he cut their noses off like Surpanakha's nose was cut off in the Ramayana. There was a legend that all those noses were put up in display cases in a secret room attached to his bedroom. I didn't know if it was true, but I had no desire to ever find out.

The guard froze in a dilemma.

Now, it was a well-known fact that Basu had a crocodile, but the fact it was named Surpanakha wasn't known to his help.

They were all forbidden to ever talk about her. I waited to see if the guard understood the fact that I knew more about their boss than they did, that I was not to be messed with.

"Yes, sir." He responded.

Good. I wouldn't have to kill him after all.

"May I know your good name, sir?" He asked, his voice polite now.

"Sheru."

He seemed skeptical, but the guard decided to leave the hard decisions to someone else. He was just going to do his job and stay out of this mess.

"Yes, sir." He replied unconvinced and walked into the guardhouse.

I positioned myself so Basu could get a clear view of my face on his screen. He would not know me, but he'd be curious to know how I knew about Surpanakha and why I had identified myself as Sheru, his arch rival and enemy.

Basu's combination of a mansion and fort was built off an old Portuguese army barracks, that he had fortified and modernized. I had seen internal video of the entire mansion through a small fly-sided flying camera we had sent inside.

I was led into the living room by two massive guards. Once in, they grabbed my arms. I didn't try to resist. That was not the point. Either I used my brains and made this work in my favor or I died here.

They pulled me towards a special metallic chair and pushed me down, and then strapped me to it with leather belts attached to it. Pretty soon, I was trussed up like a Thanksgiving Turkey, leaving them a little miffed that I had offered no resistance at all. They wanted to punch me around a little.

Basu entered the room, his Alsatian in tow. Satisfying the trope of bad men with mean looking dogs. He plopped himself down on the sofa and turned on the TV. Business channel. Hearing the market was down, Basu groaned in an exaggerated fashion and put the TV on mute.

"I'm playing with the market. Bought it down, now I'm going to buy and take it back up again. Then, I'm going to sell." Basu performed this with his hands, proud to display the power he wielded.

I didn't doubt his words. He had indirect and untraceable control of the financial brokerage firms and could bend the market to his will. After all, when all these firms reported into one man, they were essentially colluding. But there was no way to prove it. Many had tried to gather evidence, but their silence and destruction was inevitable. All Basu had to do was deliver threats to friends and families of the truth seekers.

"It was a good day today for me. My cholesterol has also gone down. But then you show up. Calling yourself a name I hate. I hate that name -

Sheru! And now, I'm in a foul mood. You know what I do when I'm in a foul mood? You know about Surpanakha. It's her lunch time. Maybe if you satisfied her appetite, that'd make me happy again. That's why you are here, you understand? To entertain me. So entertain me."

Quite a speech for Basu, but I figured he had to get it off his chest. It was probably more an explanation for his men, who didn't understand why their powerful boss was agreeing to receive a man who arrived on a bicycle. I was clearly Sudama, but to them, Basu was no Lord Krishna.

Their world would be righted when I was fed to Surpanakha. Fat chance, I thought. I was no mood to become crocodile lunch.

"Big men talk in private, Basu." I chided him.

"Big men don't arrive on small bicycles." He retorted. That bicycle thing had really hurt his ego.

"It was the only way I could get past all the army roadblocks." I responded.

I looked at the TV where the business channel was showing a small blurb on me and tying it to the idea that this might be a terrorism related event, and how that'd affect the markets. I pointed at the screen.

Basu got it then. "You are that man they are looking for."

"They were checking all the cars. They weren't looking for me on an Atlas bicycle." I said with a smile.

Basu started laughing. He loved this. He was the kind of man who loved twists in his novels, even if he liked his life to be entirely predictable from his point of view.

"You work for RAW? There's some talk of that..." he trailed off, his piercing eyes fixed on me.

"Not anymore. I was fired."

Basu started laughing again. "You know, my mood is getting better now. I think Surpanakha will have to stay hungry today."

"Oh, poor Surpanakha." I pouted. Basu laughed even more.

"Set him free. Come, you and I, we must have a drink." Then, his smile vanished. "But don't think you can try anything. Ok?"

"Basu, I'm here to talk. Not fight. I need your help. And maybe I can help you with your little problem."

"Sheru?" Basu asked.

"Who else? I have information on him that'll help you eliminate him."

"Surpanakha has been waiting for Sheru for a long time."

I smiled. He gestured to his men and they unstrapped me.

Another man had magically appeared to fix us drinks. The room was being monitored, I posited. I looked around for the camera, realizing there'd be at least five. Even if I disabled the one that could see the entrance door from where we had come in, I figured several fed directly to monitoring station with guards who'd rush in if I tried anything at all.

No, there was nothing to be done in this room. I had to get into the inner sanctum. I had to earn Basu's trust somehow.

"What kind of information are we talking about?"

"Are you sure that all of your men are trustworthy? Sure I can give you this information here with everyone listening and it won't get back to Sheru making everything I offer you worthless?"

Basu's eyes narrowed. "My men would die for me." Then he burst into laughter. "But only because I'd kill them if they refused to."

He got up. "Follow me."

The two guards walked behind me as I rubbed my wrists pretending the belts had been really tight. They hadn't. I just needed to confirm my hidden weapons, which their checks could never discover, were easily accessible. They were. I was ready.

I followed Basu. My eye fixed on the back of his neck. I followed him like a tiger follows its prey before it pounces on it, and kills it.

But things never go the way I want them to.

Blame it on Surpanakha and her nutritional needs.

TWENTY-EIGHT
A CROCK OF SHIT

I COULD NEVER GO over the image of that kid diving into a pit of shit in Slumdog Millionaire. Never could get into the movie after that point, so while the rest of the world might rave about it, I consider it a crock of shit.

I was thinking about this because here I was standing in Basu's private suite, arms outstretched while his two goons patted me down so intimately that my balls hurt after they were done, on the TV was playing "Kaun Banega Crorepati," India's adaptation of "Who wants to be a Millionaire." Basu was drinking, answering the question that the celebrity participant seemed to be stuck on.

Basu couldn't believe that the celebrity didn't know the answer to the basic question of what was at the center of an atom.

"Nucleus! Nucleus!" He yelled waving his fist at the TV, holding his glass with Glenfiddich neat in the other hand.

They finished my checks, and the two stood waiting for their boss's permission to leave.

"Did you turn on the laser beam?" He asked. They nodded yes. Basu smiled at me. So we are alone here, but there is a laser beam you will cross if you try to come to me, that'll set off alarms and when that happens, my men will reenter the room, and will simply shoot you first and ask questions later. Ok?"

I shrugged. I had no desire to be in close proximity to Basu.

The men left the room. Basu switched the TV off and turned to me, intent. "Now you talk."

I nodded, stretching out the suspense, and in my mind, calculating options as to how I could get Basu to help me with everything I needed.

"Sheru is CIA." I said it. Watched his reaction closely.

Basu opened and closed his mouth a few times, then, he laughed out loud. "Bullshit man! What bullshit!"

"I can get you proof. I can get Sheru to say to me that he is." That would get me access to equipment, travel, access to Sheru. What else did I need?

"You are lying." Basu shook his head.

"I need a gun, and grenades. Some plastic explosive."

"You are fucking lying! Wasting my time!" Basu yelled this time.

"Then shoot me dead." I yelled back.

"I have a better idea. Try and feed those lies to Surpanakha, you bastard."

Basu pressed a button and several men re-entered. The two from before grabbed each one of my arms. Basu gestured towards the far side of the room and the guards knew exactly what to do. Two ran over and separated tall curtains revealing a huge glass case containing an environment for a crocodile, including a small pond of water.

A massive Nile Crocodile slept near the water.

Surpanakha! She looked even more fearsome than I had imagined.

The two men half-dragged half-carried me towards a platform that lifted us to the top of the tank. They walked me over to the edge of the tank.

"You are lying, bastard! Admit it!" Basu spat out at me.

"Sheru is CIA. I have proof." I responded calmly.

Basu gestured with his head and the men threw me in the tank. I landed on the earth, and saw the Crocodile stir.

Basu sat down on the sofa, as one of his men handed him a drink. Another pushed a cushioned stool under his feet. Basu was setting in for the show.

I did not plan to disappoint.

"Admit you are lying. Tell me why you are really here. And my men will throw you the rope."

I looked up, sure enough, the men were holding out a rope. I smiled. I had no desire to be saved.

I walked towards the Crocodile.

Basu stopped drinking his drink, stunned by my audacity.

I got closer. The Crocodile awoke, and turned. I could tell this one was very speedy, and clearly very hungry. I doubted Basu fed it beyond what was minimally needed to keep it alive between its human feasts.

The Crocodile turned towards me, a little wary to meet someone who wasn't running away from it. It opened its mouth wide and moved a few feet towards me.

A commotion at the top of the tank took my attention away for a second. I saw a woman being lowered into the tank, hands and feet bound.

She reached the bottom and then, the rope was cut. I rushed to her. It was Sita. She opened her eyes wide in horror and I turned, just in time to see Surpanakha attack her jaws opened wide.

I slid under the croc and let its head land on me. I put my arms around it and pulled its mouth shut.

The thing with crocs is that the muscles used for opening the mouth are very weak. That allows for the mouth to be held shut. Don't ever confuse this with their bite force, which is tremendous. A force I had no desire to experience ever.

Surpanakha, taken aback at finding her mouth sealed shut by my arms proceeded to try and knock me off. She performed a death roll.

But I managed to hold on. It was a wrestling match worthy of the Gods.

I figured Basu was enjoying the show.

I had no time to wonder how Sita had ended up here. Why she was in the tank with me. I had expected my information to interest Basu, but did he already know about Sheru? Why was he so dismissive of it? He could have used this information to render Sheru untrustworthy in the underworld and eliminate him without having to lift a finger.

Surpanakha slammed me down on the ground, shaking me out of my thoughts.

I gripped her mouth tighter. She headed away from where we were, dragging me along.

Not having the advantage of seeing where we were going, I could only guess at her tactics. I didn't have to guess for long, when I suddenly found myself drowning in water. I barely had a chance to gulp in some air before I was fully underwater.

Surpanakha trashed in the water, and clearly she intended to stay there until I let her go.

Crocodiles can stay underwater for a long time, thirty minutes even.

If that was her agenda, I was certainly a dead man. My lungs were already screaming for air. It was time to change strategy.

With a bound Sita in the tank, I had no choice but to kill Surpanakha. I felt guilty about it.

I was all for Animal Rights, and to speak the truth, Surpanakha was not to blame here. It was that bastard Basu. I'd take care of him later. But for now, it was kill or be killed and I did not much care for the latter.

My right hand searched for the button on my left hand's shirt sleeve. I ripped off the button, pressed in the center to activate it. Ten seconds before it blew up. I let go of Surpanakha's mouth and she opened her mouth wide, enjoying the release.

I threw the button inside her mouth and swam below her towards her tail.

Surpanakha took a few seconds to figure out where I had gone.

I walked out of the small, artificial pond. She swung her tail but missed. I ran, away from Sita. Surpanakha turned around. Her mouth still open wide, and she raised herself on her legs and galloped towards me.

I reached the end of the tank and waited. Counting down. Four. Three. Two. One.

BOOM!

SURPANAKHA EXPLODED when she was barely three feet away from me. Her head separated and fell to the ground, her mouth still wide open. Her body continued racing towards me, the exploded neck showing the passageway into which my chunks of my flesh would have passed.

I moved to the right and her body fell to the ground, and just as quickly as it had begun, it ended.

I rushed to Sita and freed her. There was commotion on top of the tank. I figured that we'd either be shot dead now or we'd get to talk with Basu.

I was pretty happy when I realized it'd be the latter.

WE SAW Basu after getting ourselves cleaned up. It was in a different room. His eyes were red. He had been crying.

Even now, it seemed like he was on the verge of breaking down into sobs. He must have cared deeply for Surpanakha. I felt I should apologize for having blown her up.

But he stopped me with a raised palm as I started to speak. "No, it was her karma. I am sure she will be reborn as a human in her next life..." He seemed like he was about to break down again but thankfully gathered himself. Last thing I needed was a sobbing gangster.

"What next, Basu? I told you the truth, and you have a small window if you want me to find Sheru."

"She told me that you are Sheru are good friends. You came to trap me!" he screamed.

"She saw what she saw. What I'm telling you is the truth. If I had wanted to kill you, I could have used that bomb on you instead of your crocodile. I had every chance."

Basu couldn't argue against that one. I could see him thinking.

"Ok, you will get whatever you want. I don't want my name to be associated with this in any way."

"It won't. I need her to go with me."

"She dies."

"No, she will be of great help to me in delivering Sheru to you."

Basu hesitated. I could see the lust in his eyes. I saw the rage in Sita.

He must have raped her before she went into the pit, and he was clearly relishing the thought of raping her again.

"She goes with me." I said again. More than a hint of menace in my voice.

He didn't say anything more. Just nodded and waved us away.

As we left the room, I could hear the sounds of a gangster sobbing like a baby.

TWENTY-NINE
THE END OF A MARRIAGE

I MANEUVERED the Jeep out of the compound, with Sita riding shotgun. Our route snaked through quaint villages, sidestepping the main highways and their persistent roadblocks.

The Jeep was stocked: handguns and two AK-47s for defense. Sita had also procured a crate of grenades, supplementing our arsenal with several clips of ammunition.

Our journey began in silence, but as we distanced ourselves from potential surveillance, I halted the vehicle to sweep for bugs. Sita understood immediately, joining the search. Within twenty minutes, we found three bugs. One under the dash each in front of the driver and passenger seat, one under the steering wheel, and one behind the driver's seat under the leather cover.

We threw them by the side of the road and continued our journey, now with some semblance of privacy.

"I've arranged a chartered flight back to Mumbai," Sita disclosed once we were safely underway.

Her offer, while practical, left me skeptical. "I think you owe me a more comprehensive explanation before I consent to that level of confinement," I retorted with a tinge of sarcasm.

"You saved my life. I am not ungrateful."

"I saved my own life. Saving your life was an incidental."

She smiled.

"OK. We'll never be friends, but we are on the same side."

I laughed. "There are no sides, it's all one big circle."

"Yes. I'm standing next to you, willing to help you do what it is you need to." She sounded serious. I looked at her.

Sita was a beautiful woman. I had felt the attraction towards her in Sheru's place, but it was only now that I felt a certain amount of warmth towards her. I quickly shut down that line of thought. Last thing I needed. I was a man on the rebound after all.

"How did you end up with Basu?" I asked.

"He hired me. I was to pretend to be a GIP agent, and get Sheru to agree to work with us. The idea was to get his plans to eliminate Basu that we thought he'd give to the GIP. But he never got around to agreeing. Basu didn't like the fact that I had returned empty handed."

"So you are not a spy?"

"I can be whatever you want me to me."

I smiled at the way she said that.

"I'm a freelancer," she added, with a knowing smile. She was playing with me and making sure I knew it.

"So you're not a spy, just a chameleon for hire," I mused.

"You are not exactly employed anymore either, you know." she laughed. "What's the plan then?" she pressed, seeking direction.

"We'll head to Mumbai," I declared. "It's the only starting point that makes sense."

"But they'll arrest you," she warned. "You could disappear forever."

"I have no choice," I said.

"You could leave the country. I can arrange for a fake passport."

"I don't run away from trouble, Sita. I run towards it. And that's not because I'm a hero. It's because I'm stupid that way." I smiled at her.

In that moment, something shifted between her and I. She seemed to have a glow of understanding in her eyes. She nodded, smiled and touched my arm.

I wondered what that was about, but I had to give it to her. She was right. I really didn't have the next step figured out. I just wanted to get back to Mumbai and find a way to stop the assassination. Find a way to expose the takeover of RAW. Find a way to get my face off the television sets around the country. This was no way to grow my career as an deep cover intelligence agent.

Sita asked me to stop at a Chai stall we had just passed. I turned around, and she got down, saying we should get a quick drink. Sita went up to the stall owner, and he pointed inside.

Sita yelled out to me. "Come in. It's alright. They'll look after the Jeep."

I was worried about the weapons under the backseat. But I went in anyway.

Sita waited for me, then walked to the back where two men were sitting. They looked out of place and my warning signals started going off.

"They are friends, Abhay."

Sita walked over to them and they stood up, and shook hands with me. There was something about them, that stopped me from throwing a fit. Sita had meant to stop here, and had only allowed me to drive past so she could do a driveby recon.

I sat down. She sat next to me.

"You've heard about the secret group within RAW...", Sita said.

I nodded.

"We are all that remains of that group."

I let the words sink in. Did I believe her? It didn't matter what anyone said anymore, it was what they did that really had meaning.

"So you are the group that wants to kill the Prime Minister..."

"That's a bloody lie!" The tall man interrupted angrily. "It's the rogue CIA unit that will do the assassination, but they will blame it on you, a RAW operative. And then, every single change the PM set in place will get approved. That's their game plan!"

He calmed down. Then, offered his hand. "Rahul." He introduced himself. "Rahul Arora." The other man extended his hand, "Imran Khan."

I shook hands with both of them.

"And is your name really Sita?" They all laughed. Rahul piped in, "She changes her name every other week, man!"

"For now, Sita it is." She smiled at me. "We want you to join us, Abhay. You'll likely get killed if you do. But..."

I sat there, looking at this rag tag group of individuals, and for the first time ever in my life, I didn't feel alone.

I smiled. For the world was a good place.

"Priyanka... your wife. She's with them, right?" Sita asked.

I thought for a moment before I said "She's not my wife anymore."

We stepped out of the Dhaba to find several army men surrounding our jeep. I felt my heart sink. This was it, we weren't getting out of this one.

One of the army men, a Gurkha Sergeant, walked up to us. To me. His eyes blazed with anger and if looks could kill, he would already have had several times over.

Sita put her hand out and he stopped.

"He's a friend," she told him.

He looked confused. "But..." he began, then trailed off. "If you say he's a friend, then, he is a friend."

He stretched out his hand. I shook it. He saluted us, and turned around and commanded his men, "Company! Back to base!"

He turned back one more time and spoke to us all, but Sita mostly. It was clear she was the unspoken leader of the group.

"If you never need any help, Madam, please just let me know."

Sita smiled. "Thank you, Bahadur."

Sergeant Harikishen Bahadur walked away to his Jeep, and soon the contingent of Army men was gone.

Rahul and Imran got in the Jeep with us. They had gotten here hitching rides. Rahul insisted on driving, so Sita and I sat in the back.

We headed to the airport.

I prayed Sita wouldn't notice me stealing glances at her, driven by a strange, deep longing growing in my soul.

THIRTY
REAWAKENINGS

DURING THE FLIGHT back to Mumbai, Rahul, Imran, Sita, and I pored over the intelligence we'd pooled.

But it took a call from one of the group's informers within RAW who revealed the fact that the RAW appointments were already in place. A news leak had prompted some rumblings on the so-called arbitrary changes. The PM had released a note through his spokesperson that all changes were very well-considered, approved by everyone that needed to approve them, and could not be further discussed due to National Security concerns. These changes, he insisted, were due to infiltration of the security apparatus by enemy agents, and this was the right thing to do.

His admission that the RAW agency had been infiltrated had raised a hue and cry, but the political player that the PM was, he kept the focus off the appointments, and managed to keep the conversation about something else.

We now knew that the assassination of the PM would be pinned on a RAW agent. This meant that the PM would be assassinated much earlier than his visits to the zoo or the university. Those options were diversions, keeping us focused on a later timeline than the actual one.

It hit me then that anything on the PM's official schedule was not going to be the valid target list. They would need that info in a place that only I'd have access to.

So I hacked back into my RAW secure account. I started a search on my remote desktop and sure enough, hidden away in a deep folder was a schedule for the PMs personal appointments. That should never have been on my computer, so it was clearly planted to implicate me after the assassination.

I scoured his personal appointments and found he was scheduled for a personal trip to the Delhi Gurdwara on the anniversary of Guru Nanak Dev Ji, founder of the Sikh religion.

The PM, who was a Sikh, rarely made any noise about his religious beliefs. It made sense that this appointment would not appear on his official calendar but would be an unspoken agreement between his assistant and himself, that nothing important would be scheduled on this day.

The date of the Guru Nanak Dev Ji's birthday varies year to year based on the traditional Indian calendar. This year the date fell on November 28th, which was two days from now. We decided the best thing to do was to go to Delhi.

Imran walked over to the cockpit and informed the pilots of our desire to go to Delhi instead. We had sufficient fuel onboard, and the pilots rerouted to Delhi midair.

We reached Delhi in an hour and half. Another half an hour later, we were ensconced in a room at The Connaught Palace, which was a stone's throw from the very busy Connaught Circle and the Gurdwara Sis Ganj.

WE SPLIT INTO TWO GROUPS.

Sita and Rahul would stay in the room and brainstorm the attack vectors, then recce the neighborhood to validate and prioritize. The constraining principle was that the assassin would have to successfully kill the PM and not be caught or identified. This was the only way to implicate me as being the assassin. This ruled out several attack vectors.

Imran and I would recce the surrounding area with a view to determine the holding location for the assassin or assassins. They were probably holed up in a similar location to ours.

Imran and I decided to visit the Gurdwara first and get the lay of the land starting from there. We went around the Gurdwara, sans footwear which was left outside, and a colorful handkerchief sized cloth covering our head.

The crowd was thin. Several men we thought belonged to the PMs security contingent were present in regular attire, in preparation for the upcoming visit by the PM.

This was not a public visit, so the PM would arrive with a very small contingent, offer his prayers and leave. There was a separate entrance for officials which lead directly to the center of the Gurdwara.

The security would be minimal and discreet so as to not attract attention. The PM was in a difficult spot and any display of religion would give his opponents an opportunity to tie him to the resurgence of the Khalistan issue. Pre-election, this was not something he'd want.

We were sans our weapons.

We had completed recceing the first two levels of the Gurdwara, when I saw her.

Priyanka.

She had her back to me, but her walk was unmistakable. She was wearing a Shalwar-Kameez, and a shawl to cover her head. She turned and started walking towards us, head bowed. I nudged Imran and nodded in her direction. Imran quickly moved to cover me. We let her pass, then continued walking in case she had a partner watching her tail.

I didn't see Sheru or anyone who seemed to be focused on her. Imran and I turned around and followed her.

"Do you want to capture her?" Imran asked.

"Why not? We have to thrown a wrench in their plans. It's our only chance of thwarting them."

"If they get alerted to our presence...?" Imran wondered, unsure of my plan. "We should call Sita and ask her."

"No time to do that." I decided to shut down his indecision and sped up. I'd take Priyanka down no matter what. In many ways, she was the mission. She had started all this. Many years ago.

All the years of my life that I had lost. Priyanka had to answer for them. I felt like I had been living a bad dream. But I was awake now. And I wanted answers.

PRIYANKA WAS MOVING FASTER NOW. Had she seen us? Was that why she had her head down? I didn't care. There was no way she was getting away from me now.

Imran kept up with me, trying hard not to be obvious about it. "I really think we should call Sita." he insisted. My ears were deaf to everything except the searing questions I was going to ask Priyanka.

We reached the ground floor. Priyanka was already at the gate.

I started running, immediately attracting stares from the other visitors at the Gurdwara. People tensed up. This kind of an event was not welcome at a Gurdwara. Thankfully, I managed to reach the gate before anyone could interfere.

Imran reached me a few moments later as I looked around for Priyanka. I saw her first. She was walking into an alley. And just before she disappeared around the corner, she turned.

Our eyes locked. She knew! Dammit, she knew!

I broke into a run. Imran right at my side. We entered the alley in pursuit. Priyanka raced around a corner and disappeared.

"Imran, go right! Cut her off!" Imran peeled away. I turned the corner and came to a quick stop.

Priyanka stood in front of me. We looked at each other for what seemed an eternity. Finally, I saw the Glock in her hand. Aimed squarely at my heart. I scoffed.

"What are you waiting for? Pull the trigger, Priyanka." Her name dripped from my mouth like venom.

"You can't stop this, Abhay. There are too many people, powerful people, who want this."

"Well, they can't have it now, can they?" My face had turned to stone.

"Even if you stop them here, they'll still get what they want. But you will die."

"Them? Aren't you one of them?" I dared her to say no. Dared her to try and fool me again.

"I'm sorry, Abhay. I'm so sorry."

"Give me the gun." I softened my tone a little. I needed her alive.

I saw Imran turn the corner and approach. Priyanka saw my gaze shift and smiled.

"How close is he?" She asked.

I turned back to her. She knew about Imran too.

"Give me the gun, Priyanka, and I swear, for the times we shared, for the good times we did have, you'll not be killed."

"I'm already dead, Abhay. I died a long time ago."

I rushed her. Maybe I saw it in her sad smile, or I saw it in her eyes, but I saw it before she even raised the gun. But I was too late.

Priyanka switched her aim from me, to her temple.

She pulled the trigger.

Her lifeless body fell, her eyes still fixed on me.

A small sad smile on her lips. My world crashed to the ground with Priyanka's dead body.

I didn't see the car pull up. I didn't see Rahul and Sita run up to us. I didn't see Rahul and Imran rush to lift Priyanka's body...

I saw nothing until Sita closed the eyelids on those eyes that had lost their life.

It was in that moment I realized I had loved Priyanka.

I had always loved her. And what killed my soul in that moment was that I realized Priyanka had loved me too.

THIRTY-ONE
THE END OF EVERYTHING

THE AFTERMATH of the gunshot swiftly brought news crews flocking to the vicinity of the Gurdwara. The Prime Minister's visit was hastily canceled; he opted to pray elsewhere, averting any assassination attempt there.

The PM's recent appointments had stirred the Lok Sabha into an uproar. Leaks, facilitated by Imran and amplified by Rahul's media savvy, sowed doubts about the PM "selling" our intelligence to outside interests.

A detailed list of the corrupt officers picked to head RAW, and tapes of their indiscretions were found in a hotel room, the key to which was in Priyanka's pocket.

In the end, Priyanka had helped save India from the plot against it.

Sita's guess was that Priyanka was deep cover RAW, but we'd never know now. I gained no comfort from that thought.

Sita had arranged for Priyanka's body to be carried away before the police had gotten there. She made it clear that there was no purpose to letting them have Priyanka's body. We'd cremate it in private with the respect she deserved, having done what she had done. The ashes would be given to me. After all, I was still her husband.

I watched Priyanka's body being consumed by the flames.

That night, I had a dream that I have never had before. In my dream, I was back in Hyderabad, and had stolen a pedal rickshaw, and was driving down a familiar childhood street in the locality called Narayanguda when I saw an old friend crossing the street. I had meant to meet him but had not gotten around to doing so. And so, when I randomly saw him on the road, I got very excited. I parked the stolen rickshaw and yelled out to him as he crossed the road. "Sanjay!"

He turned, recognizing his name, but he didn't seem to recognize me. With an embarrassed look, he started walking away from me, and before I could stop him, had jumped on the pillion seat behind someone riding a Vespa scooter and was gone before I could stop him.

I ran after him. But the roads changed. There was new construction everywhere. I got to the place where his house used to be, but now, there stood a tall apartment building with countless units. I realized I would never be able to find him.

I decided to go to an old library I frequented, wanting to get some novels for my dad to read. But for reasons I didn't remember after I woke up, that didn't happen either.

Unusual dreams of unfinished business, of old friends, departed family, missed opportunities. Priyanka and I would always be unfinished business. Dreams now my only connection to closure.

I lay in bed for a long time, unable to move.

Eventually, I got out of bed and made coffee for myself.

ALL LANDINGS ARE CONTROLLED CRASHES.

Two massive objects collide.

Planet Earth, the more massive one. The plane not as massive, but an object still larger than our beings.

I always marveled at the combination of aerodynamics that kept the plane afloat, the glide path that provided a safe angle to hit the ground with, the wheel that turned the moment of contact into an agreeable event for the plane. Such marvelous inventions and combined in ways probably not predicted by any of their original inventors, or should that be discoverers?

I felt small.

I was living on the shoulders of giants, who in turn were as small as small can be. I wondered about our place in the universe. About the games we played as intelligence agents. I wondered what it all amounted to.

My recurring dream of being in a plane that was about to land, and ends up doing so in an unexpected place.

In one dream, it had landed on a market road in Hyderabad having missed the approach into the Hyderabad airport.

We missed a lamppost, traffic, and had slow-moving buffalos in front of us as the pilot began to taxi back to the airport.

This very small jet had suddenly become like a car. A guy appeared out of nowhere, acting as a conductor would do on the state transport buses, shouting at the indifferent traffic to move out of the way of the taxiing plane, so we could get back to the airport. The dream ended with moments of meeting my wife, my two daughters.

Perhaps it was a glimpse of a parallel universe. I had no one in this life. Priyanka was gone. She was the only chance I ever truly had of creating family.

Back to reality.

I was onboard a Citation Jet and looked out the window as it taxied towards the runway. I imagined the pilots running through their checklists. Doing their job. Like I had to do mine when I reached my destination.

My thoughts turned back to my dreams. Another recurring dream about being on a bicycle seat that was so high, higher than the tallest trees, and the power cables even. I'd see the people far down below and wonder how I'd stop, how I'd get down, and how I'd avoid those power cables that were sure to electrocute me.

Are our dreams just random neural activity, or if they were the genetic legacy of our forefather's terrors, reinterpreted by our brain within the context of our current experiences. If this was true, my forefathers clearly used to piss their pants a lot. I mean, a lot.

I suppose everyone on a plane has anxious moments when it's about to land. It was a surprise that all that anxiety and that programmed response we had of imagining all the possible scenarios, mostly negative ones, didn't create a negative field around the plane.

Enough to actually make those negative scenarios come true. Perhaps human thought does not actually control reality, no matter what the 'positive thinking' crowd wants you to believe.

As anxious a moment a landing can be, takeoffs are no less anxious.

Yes, we are separating from a solid object, and the feeling is one of safety, but deferred disaster. The truth is that takeoffs can be a very risky affair too. There is, after all, the long journey to the destination, during which anything can happen.

I wondered what this takeoff, and this journey would be like.

I sat back in seat Bravo Three. My seatbelt fastened, my tray table stowed, and my seat back in upright position as the Citation trundled down the runway gathering up speed.

Soon it reached the point of no return. No aborted landing possible now. We had to takeoff or crash. I hoped for the former. The Citation reached V0 and the nose pulled up.

We headed out west, leaving behind the coastline of Mumbai with the orangish-yellow lights dotting the coastal roadways, and embracing the darkness of the Arabian Sea. Like in life, only the occasional set of lights belonging to ships sailing in the night broke the darkness. The only other respite from the inky blackness came as you looked out to the horizon where the sky merged with the land, and the sparse blanket of stars began.

We are afraid of darkness. There is a lot more darkness in this universe than there is light, but possibly no place darker than the soul of man. Like the sailor sailing these seas looked to the stars to guide him or her, I held the distant stars in my gaze, hoping they'd guide me to a destination that was filled with light and joy.

I wanted to leave behind the world of despair and darkness.

Unfortunately for me, what I wanted and what I got, have always been two very different things.

ABOUT THE AUTHOR

Nikhil Kamkolkar is a writer-filmmaker and **Unreal Authorized Instructor (Gold)** blending story, cinematography, and real-time tech. An **Unreal Engine Animation Fellowship** alum, he works across development, previs, and final pixels, and is in pre-production on a sci-fi short that integrates Unreal with emerging AI workflows.

He wrote and directed the feature rom-com **LOVE LOVE** (streaming globally on Amazon Prime, HOOPLA, and more), plus award-winning shorts.

His TV pilots (sci-fi, horror, thriller) have placed in **Screencraft** and **Final Draft Big Break**. Alongside filmmaking, he's held day-job roles at **Microsoft, MTV, Nickelodeon,** and **Topic**. Several of his screenplays are published as books on major retailers.

Based in New Jersey and working internationally, he focuses on filmmaker practice, creative resilience, and real-time/AI tooling.

More at **KAM9.TV**.

instagram.com/nikhilnyc
facebook.com/nikhilkamkolkar
tiktok.com/@kam9tv

ALSO BY NIKHIL KAMKOLKAR

LOVE LOVE: Screenplay by Nikhil Kamkolkar (Rising Stakes Screenplay Series)

Short Film Scripts: By Nikhil Kamkolkar (Rising Stakes Screenplay Series)

RAW Deception: Novelization of a screenplay (Rising Stakes Screenplay Series)

3 SHORT STORIES: Adapted from Short Film Screenplays (Rising Stakes Screenplay Series)

LOVE LOVE: From Fantasy to Forever (Motion Picture)

Streaming on Amazon Prime, HOOPLA and others.

LOVE LOVE: Archivum 2059 (Motion Picture)

Coming Soon

LEAVE A REVIEW

IF THIS BOOK HELPED, A SHORT HONEST REVIEW REALLY HELPS OTHER READERS DISCOVER IT. THANK YOU.
